# *Agatta*

A Novel By

Cathy Clay

Veritable Clay

Houston

♠

Publisher's Note:
This book is a work of fiction. Names, characters, places, and incidents are either the product of the author's imagination or are used fictitiously, and any resemblance to actual persons, living or dead, events, or locales is entirely coincidental.



ISBN 978-0-9761352-0-3

All scriptures are quoted from the Authorized King James Version of the Holy Bible.

# Contents

# Acknowledgment

I have much gratitude for my family; without them this journey would have been far more difficult, if not altogether impossible. Moreover, I am forever indebted to the characters in this novel for allowing me to be a vessel for the telling of their stories. Also I greatly appreciate the scholars and mentors who have encouraged my endeavors. Most of all, I thank the Lord for guiding me through this project every step of the way.

*To my family*

The thing that hath been, it *is that* which shall be; and that which is done *is* that which shall be done: and *there is* no new *thing* under the sun.

—Ecclesiastes 1:9

Agatta Lugar arrived at No. 51 Dauphine Street, Madam Zulime Clovis's Bordello, in 1884 on Valentine's Day; she was fourteen years old. Since then, three years had passed and she had become one of Clovis's most prosperous harlots. Specializing in women of color, Madam Clovis had operated a successful New Orleans assignation house for seventeen years. With Agatta as a prized acquisition, her trade grew all the more lucrative for the latter of her reign.

Standing five feet seven inches tall, with a svelte hourglass figure, Agatta's charms were unrivaled. Onyx almond shaped eyes, an aquiline nose, and a full African mouth with a deep sensuous Cupid's bow composed her regal mahogany face. A birthmark, a few shades darker than her coloring and the size of a ten-cent piece adorned the center of her forehead. All crowned by a mass of lustrous raven hair.

Veiled by a light haze of early morning fog, the Vieux Carré manifested as a mirage. Moisture ripened the smell of horses, and dampened their coats. With glistening dew-drenched manes, they appeared both majestic and mythical. French Market patrons gathered under the barracks to barter over the abundant assortment of fruits, vegetables, spices, and preserves. Fancy men, painted ladies, tailors, seamstresses, maids, and housewives were drawn to the fathomless array of imported gabardines, silks, satins, and velvets. A peculiar harmony of diverse languages simultaneously flowed through crowded isles. Inflections of French, Creole, Spanish, English, and Italian produced poetry of wildly exuberant lyrics. All kinds of healers from confidence men to shaman touted potions, spells, and talismans to cure every human affliction. Street performers played banjoes, washboards, harmonicas, pots, and pans. The rattle-tin sounds of their coins landing into cups and buckets accompanied their music. Worshippers went to mass at St. Louis Cathedral. Some traveled by carriage or wagon; most strolled along with family and friends. Bartenders, saloonkeepers, and barmaids splashed the sidewalks with pails of water to rid Sunday morning of Saturday night's stench. Alluring harlots of every hue lined the balconies of Conti Street. Cooling themselves with decorative fans, they flirtatiously waived clients good-bye while sparking the interests of new prospects. Madams and pimps graced thresholds for formal farewells.

Agatta strolled; content with her purchases and daydreaming about the power of appeal once she donned them. Her boxes contained brightly colored stockings, intricately laced garters, brocade corsets, silk nightgowns, lace-trimmed drawers, and petticoats. Like all the women of No. 51, she was well attired.

Thus far 1887 had been cordial. Oddly enough, it was February again. Although the wind still had a biting chill, winter would soon give way to the prelusive warmth that nurtured renewal and maturation. Agatta turned onto Dauphine. The skirt of her crimson dress flowed about her ankles as though trying to circumvent a phantom. Cloaked in her mysterious air, she seemed to be ever moving toward something—higher. Through the course of her journey, men were incessantly drawn to her mystique.

Two fellows walking toward Agatta tipped their hats. One of them remarked, "That's something else."

As she neared No. 51, she noticed one of Sazar's girls watching her from a balcony. She strutted about with one hand on her hip, twisting her blazing hair. A sorry effort at mock confidence since her eyes gave her away. If they were the windows to the soul, then she harbored enough sorrow to trigger heart failure.

Resting on one of two verdigris griffins perched on either side of No. 51's steps, Zulime saw their silent exchange. When she had Agatta's attention, she offered a message of her own: You better watch out for that one.

With a smile and a nod of respect, Agatta acknowledged the warning. That woman don't miss nothing, she thought.

Although Zulime had reached the middle sector of her years, there wasn't a line in her face to condemn her. A generous bustline and wide hips rounded out her small stature, and agreed with her authoritative air. Today her ruddy hair was coiffed in an upsweep. An emerald green wool dress and a large cameo at her collar completed her dignified Sunday style. When she smiled, dimples in her tawny cheeks turned her into a jovial diva. The twinkling brown eyes, however, indicated smarts that had better not be taken lightly.

She had left Baton Rouge during the early 1860s. Her parents were schoolteachers and devout Christians. Her mother, Ines, was born free to modest farmers. Basil Clovis, Zulime's father, had been a slave; but with money that he earned as a carpenter, he purchased his and his mother's freedom. He learned to read and completed his studies at the Institute for Colored Youth. Basil was high on God, hard on mere mortals, and blessed with a steel will that he believed everyone should aspire to; especially his daughters, Zulime and Emily. "Sin will keep you longer than you're willing to stay," were his last words to Zulime. After burying a stillborn baby girl and divorcing an unfaithful potter, she wasn't willing to stay in Baton Rouge. So she followed her lover, Valor Gatlin, a handsome white gambler, to New Orleans.

She lived as a *secretly* kept woman. Which was often a lonely existence, when Valor was away living white or chasing big games throughout the South. With the turbulence of the war, jobs were few. To ward off loneliness and learn the city,

Zulime did stints as a cook, tarot card reader, and waitress. One day out of the blue, Valor gave her twenty thousand dollars, kissed her hand, and disappeared. She used some of the newfound wealth to purchase and refurbish No. 51.

Over time she acquired her own wealth. By way of sheer dauntlessness, she achieved staying power. Respected by people in her trade as a quick-witted, shrewd, flamboyant madam who flaunted big jewels, housed the prettiest harlots in New Orleans in a showplace bordello, charged top dollar, and managed her profits well. Revered by her girls, she shared close relationships with a few, among them Agatta.

"Morning lady," Zulime said, in a low voice.

"Morning, Mam. Looks like an easy Sunday."

"Ought to be. We had a hell of a Saturday. I'm going to the room. You want tea?"

"Yeah, I'll put away my things."

An understated eroticism prevailed at No. 51. Two bronze blackamoor statues flanked the parlor entrance. A six-arm brass chandelier lit the room. A tapestry colored of passionate reds ranging from rose to magenta covered the West wall. Its weave portrayed the spectrum of purple arts. The other walls showcased a gallery of paintings and photographs depicting semi-nude to elaborately dressed women. Two mahogany camelback sofas covered in luxurious burgundy velvet faced each other with a black marble fruitwood table between them. Side tables, a recamier, a pair of Rococo Revival chairs, and a lyre-form settee comprised the rest of the parlor furnishings. Ivies grew lush and long from hanging pots. Gardenias bloomed from porcelain pots. Incensed burned fragrantly throughout the ground floor. Seamlessly everything worked together to create an elegant bewitching ambience.

Waiting for Zulime, Agatta peered over the banister.

The room was the attic. It served as a place for prayer, meditation, or solitude. Rosaries, candles, and the Holy Bible were on the console table. A wooden cross hung centered above, between an icon of Saint Christopher, patron saint of travelers; and an etching of the prophet Hosea. The girls referred to the room with its veritable altar as Mam's church. The fact that is existed at all was simply "Mam's way."

They knew what her way was. All of them had been exposed to religion, some more than others. With clarity they remembered holiness from the women who shared their bloodlines. Every now and then they saw righteousness in themselves and their sisters at No. 51. Many of them had tried to bury their faith because they felt ruined, filthy, and cast off; therefore no longer worthy of God's grace. Moreover, faith was an entity connected to a masculine force; such forces constantly took from them but never lingered for long. Thus, they trusted God just not too much. They accepted that ideology because it set them free enough to be whores. Yet when in need, they knew that faith was close by (near miracle). So they kept their holy of holies tucked away; to be fully resurrected when they got ready or got right.

Zulime understood all of that. Often she found the room holier than she left it. Tearstained handkerchiefs, lone flowers, wrinkled letters, faded photographs, blessed oil, singed locks of hair, a chair rocking, warm candles, and the lingering spirit of brokenness were telltale signs.

Agatta held the door for Zulime, who carried a tea tray. Chamomile infused the air as they filled their cups.

Agatta managed to open the attic's tiny window, which was stiffened by time. As dust flew everywhere, she coughed and fanned wildly. The influx of fresh air was worth the trouble. She took her cup and settled in the rocking chair.

Sipping, Zulime relaxed on the chaise and searched her mind for something that might encourage Agatta to share her past. No one knew what led her to the cold wet alley where Grace and Magdalena had found her. For all their fondness, Agatta remained a woman with no yesterdays.

"Time is something else ain't it?" Zulime said.

"Watching the sunlight bathe the oyster-colored walls, Agatta rocked slowly. "If that's all you need."

"That's never *all* you need. Time helps you see things much clearer. It can put plenty distance between where you used to be and where you are."

"I don't know about that."

Zulime drank the last of her tea, and asked, "Do you want to?"

"What difference does it make?"

"A big one. Time is like faith. It'll heal you, if you let it."

"Time can't heal everything . . . it don't change nothing." Agatta sat her cup down, went to the window, and watched the passersby.

"Dolin', you don't have to carry your burdens forever."

"I'm not ready Mam. Please don't push me."

Magdalena Marie cracked the door and peeked inside. Two dark pigtails dusting her buttermilk shoulders and pouting pink lips bespoke innocence, but the soft plump breasts under the nightgown signaled siren. "Morning, y'all seen Grace?"

Agatta turned around and answered, "She left early this morning—in a hurry like."

"Come sit, cher." Zulime invited.

"No thank you. I got plenty to do."

"You have the whole day."

"I rather get an early start."

Twiddling her thumbs, Zulime said, "Got word you rode off to Algiers with Numa Sabatier the other day."

With her hands on her hips, Magdalena stepped inside the attic. "Who I ride off with is my business."

"True. But your man loves lady luck, and she don't return the favor. Half the hustlers in Nawlins' ready to open his throat. Just be careful."

"I been caring for myself a long time."

"Reckon you have, but that don't mean you know everything."

"I know enough."

"Do you know how to love a man and still see his faults?"

"Who and how I love is my business." Magdalena bit the inside of her lip and sighed. "I 'preciate if you stay in your place."

Raising her hands, Zulime retorted, "This is my place."

"Yeah it is, and one day I'm gon' leave way from here running and never look back."

"Sister, that's fine by me. I just hope you know what you're running to."

"Let me handle that. In the meantime, I can't sit here and play church with you." Magdalena left, jerking the door behind her.

"Mam."

"Yeah."

Looking out the window again, Agatta asked, "Why you care so much about what we do? How we feel? What manner of fortune we find?"

"I'd hate to come all this way and never care about nobody."

"Umh."

"I hear you found somebody to care for too."

Grinning, Agatta folded her arms and turned to Zulime. "Somebody found me."

# 2

## The History of Sazar Jorda

Sorrow *is* better than laughter: for by the sadness of the countenance the heart is made better.

—Ecclesiastes 7:3

Canal Street bustled with activity. Blowing steam, driving thoroughbreds, and rattling all the way, the streetcar transported passengers to the commercial district. Vendors cried out and rang triangles or sounded off tin horns to advertise hot foods. Fried oysters and shrimp, stuffed fish, and cakes were mouthwatering staples. Confidence men wearing frayed musty suits and weather-beaten hats peddled the quintessential snake oil, guaranteed to chase away worries, cure physical afflictions, and manifest bonuses of love and money blessings. They pitched a sale to anybody who passed by: melancholy children, old folks on wobbly canes, hobos, Chantilly lace clad ladies, and men with impeccably groomed handlebar mustaches. Fervent evangelists passed out Bibles, prayed, and warned that these were the last days.

Among the multitudes, an aloof, six feet tall native New Orleanian stood below a cast iron gallery on Touro Row. He had just visited the realtor, and secured another property in the colored neighborhood of the Faubourg Tremé. Carefully he folded the deed and tucked it in his coat pocket. He licked his forefinger then ran it across a dark tapered wave near his temple. Beckoned by the sights and sounds, he gazed out at the street, and started down the walk.

His attention did not drift from side to side, nor into the lustful stares that fell upon him. Concerned only with spending the afternoon with his lover, he looked straight ahead toward the route that would lead him to her. A pimp by profession, romantic by calling; every rumor from cold-blooded outlaw to stone cold gentleman surrounded him. The story depended upon the orator. Yet most of the tales about Sazar Jorda bent toward infamy.

A Creole of color, his was an arresting beauty. Cooler temperatures had faded his light complexion to the hue of a honeydew melon. A slight slant distinguished his piercing dark eyes. A keen nose denoted an aristocratic air. An Ibo pout left his mouth to fall shy of thin. High cheekbones and an angular jawline marked the gorgeous symmetry of his face.

A dark custom-made suit beautifully draped Sazar's well-formed physique. A crisp white shirt and a silk prism patterned grey vest fit his broad shoulders and taut torso flawlessly. For all the scandalous talk, Sazar was pure pleasure to the eyes.

A perpetual daydreamer, on a lively day like this Monday, his mind was apt to wander. Scenes, both familiar and sacred, sent his thoughts on a fantastic tangent to the past. A past woven with bliss, loss, and a love to live for.

Steamships lined the riverfront blowing smoke into the clear blue yonder. Like black magic, the haloes of industry got to him every time. Stevedores transported cargo to and from the Mississippi jewels. Whereas the riverfront alone was enough to trigger his mind's eye, there was another catalyst—Agatta. Maybe it was her fragility, or her quiet temperament, or the assurance that his search for sublime love was over. Perhaps it was her resemblance to his mother. Whatever it was, no single key unlocked Sazar's history coffer.

His thoughts scurried a little, but he knew beforehand that they would settle in 1867. For that was a year of irrevocable change; a season that cast the dye for his destiny. That it was twenty years ago did not matter; the seventh year of his life remained as near to him as his pulse.

Alex and Rose Jorda were equally yoked and divinely in love. They were highly attuned to each other's needs, ways, and desires. Although their romance retained an element of possessiveness, it also entailed a remarkable measure of trust. Praise to one was homage to the other.

Alex had been born in New Orleans. His parents were free people of color who had fled Santo Domingo as children during the Haitian Revolution. In 1859, Alex and his father were visiting relatives in Jefferson Parish when he saw an intriguing lithe figure shucking peas on her grandmother's porch. Alex decided then and there that he would have and hold the cinnamon doll for the rest of his days.

The tall confident sailor surpassed the young Rose LaPomeret's prayers. What a blessing for her to be sitting because her knees waxed soft at first sight of him. One look into his light grey eyes, and she wanted to see the sunrise on his handsome café au lait face, and kiss his tenuous stern lips forever. There was not a single thing about him that Rose could not love; his striking profile made her think of a crescent moon. A pointed nose hinted arrogance, but he greeted folks with ease and looked them in the eyes. Rightly, she pegged him worldly; after all, he was from New Orleans, a seaman, and nine years her senior.

Alex asked Adele LaPomeret for Rose's hand. She blessed them and aired out her wedding dress. Within four days, Alex had taken a fifteen-year-old bride, and they were headed home to build and share a life in New Orleans.

The couple had few friends. Both were somewhat reserved. Besides, marriage filled their cups. When Alex was onshore, which totaled about six months out of the year, he and Rose spent most of their time together. They enjoyed long walks, dancing, theater, and shopping. Each of them, however, had one close friend.

Mr. Joseph Anthony and Alex had grown up together, but Mr. Anthony looked at least a decade older than Alex. By the age of thirty, his curly, once black hair had turned silver, and shined like new money next to his bronze skin. His build was staunch; brawn earned from hard labor. Cocky to a fault, he had a swagger to his gait. Sazar liked listening to Mr. Anthony talk. His voice was scratchy. When he spoke English, he held his words like a balladeer; but when he conversed in Creole, he spoke fast and fluently. In either language, Sazar gathered that his father and Mr. Anthony had run wild as boys. Life at sea provided and oasis for their adventurous spirits.

An elderly woman, Miss Irene, was Rose's dearest friend. Although Rose never said so, Sazar assumed that the two women had known each other from Jefferson Parish. They got along fondly, like people with a shared history. Often they would sit on the gallery laughing and talking until sundown. Sometimes they behaved like mother and daughter. Rose would wash and braid Miss Irene's hair, and help her with cooking and cleaning.

Above friendship, but below marriage was Sazar, the Jorda's only child. Both parents joyfully invested energy and affection in their progeny. Alex sparked his son's interest in foreign lands. By sharing fascinating stories of his travels to Europe, South America, and the Caribbean, he taught his son that their world was not *the world.* Sports were more than mere amusement for the Jorda men. Croquet and fishing offered a wellspring of opportunities for Alex to shape and mold Sazar's character while bonding with him. One needed skill to drive away an opponent's ball, preparation to bait a hook, and patience to wait for a catch. True to his calling, Alex owned an extensive collection of model ships; the majority of which were souvenirs from his travels. He encouraged Sazar to take up the hobby by hunting and gathering a small fleet for him; though the boy enjoyed his marble collection far more. Ever enamored with music, Alex played the guitar with the ease of a virtuoso, and frequently gave lessons to a less enthused Sazar. Yet of all the activities that father and son shared together, a dark sky reigned as the wonder of all wonders. Many a night, celestial bodies harkened them to spend hours gazing through a telescope. Somehow the Big Dipper made it plausible that God knew man before the foundation of the world. Coincidentally, Alex's interests appealed to Sazar's curiosity and sense of adventure; whereas Rose's inclinations spoke to his introspective intellectual side.

She fostered his appreciation for literature. At bedtime or around the fireplace, her mellow voice read dime novels or the works of William Shakespeare, John Milton, and John Donne. She poured enough Scripture into Sazar for him to know the Ten Commandments and the Lord's Prayer by heart at the age of four. Art was another of Rose's passions, and Sazar tagged along on her countless excursions to local shops and markets to rummage for pictures. In support of her pursuits for lovely images, Alex brought home original works from the ports he traveled. Framed paintings and drawings were tastefully displayed on the walls of their abode. Sazar absorbed all the gifts and influences his parents bestowed upon him; the Jorda's most profound impressions, however, were that of love, devotion, and sacrifice.

Alex hurried down the levee to where Rose and Sazar were. He took off his hat and waved merrily, overcome with joy that he would remain onshore for the entire summer. He embraced Rose, lifting her off the ground. Playfully, he swung her around then put her down to step back and take a look at her. Rose held back tears of joy, and fell into his arms for a lasting kiss. "I missed you girl," he said, his hands slipped to her waist.

"Welcome home Papa," she whispered. She backed away and steered Sazar toward his father.

Alex bent down, mussed his son's hair, and pecked him on the forehead. "You take good care of your mama lil' man?"

"Always, Papa."

"Très bien."

"Tell me about the sail."

"We have all day for that. Later on, I'll take you on board. How 'bout that?"

"Merci!"

"Your world enchants him," Rose said.

"Our boy's given to fancy. Many things enchant him." Alex took Rose by the hand. The three of them started toward their home in the

Tremé. "You enchant me, my dear. I must admit—I missed you madly."

"Madly?"

"Like I was 'bout to lose my mind."

She giggled.

"We came across some rough waters sailing through Grenada. I thought we might not make it. Lord, how I prayed."

"He heard you. Sailing's in your blood. The danger draws you."

"I know dolin', but love draws me home. I look forward to staying home for good someday."

"That day's a ways off."

"I'm counting on it."

"Me too," Rose said.

They approached the pretty pink cottage on Marais in with its arched windows and dark grey shutters. Inside light bounced off the stucco walls, and made some of the faces in the paintings look as though they were laughing.

Alex hung his coat and hat then disappeared to the rear of the house. Rose went to the kitchen, and returned with a slice of rum cake folded in a napkin. "Go on the gallery while I bathe Papa."

"Yes ma'am." Sazar ran to the study and grabbed a picture book off the shelf then went outside and sat on the steps.

He licked icing off his fingers as he watched a wasp circling the blooming coral tree. June 3 was warm but liberal breezes made it sweet enough to curl up and take a nap, but Sazar had other plans. He opened the book and browsed pages of ships;

fascinated by their sizes, hiding places, their ability to take him afar, and best of all—his father worked on one.

Board and anxious, Sazar closed the book, shoved the napkin in his pocket, and waited. He gave his parents enough time to grow comfortable in their privacy before taking his shoes off and tiptoeing back into the house. He slipped inside, careful not to let the door make a sound.

He crept past the drawing room, past his room, and past the dining room through the rear door, which opened to a courtyard that separated the main house from the kitchen, where his parents were. Peeking through the leaves of a large banana palm, he viewed them.

Alex rested in a large tin tub while Rose prepared his bath. She returned with the last pail of water from the cistern. She knelt down, rolled her sleeves further up, and poured soap into Alex's hair. Vigorously she lathered then slowly she poured water over his head. She took a towel and tenderly dried his hair and face. He closed his eyes and relaxed his shoulders as Rose began to bathe him. "You get better and better at this," he moaned.

"I know no greater joy than serving you. Believe me when I say your absence leaves me to fret."

"Show me." Alex removed the pin from Rose's hair, leaving soft thick black curls to spring out past her chin. She cast her clothing and shoes aside. Holding Alex's hands, she lowered herself on top of him. Ardently they kissed and caressed. After some tossing, she rested beneath him, submerging her torso in the warm water. Her gaze stayed upon him, and like a man who had been kept from his wife a lifetime and promised her in the next, he entered her. "Dear, Rose . . . sweet lady Rose," he bellowed.

Sazar came from behind the tree and moved in closer, hoping that proximity might unravel the mystery of covenant romance. Stunned by his mother's electrifying sensuality and infallible charms. The effects of which mesmerized his father, leaving the man to quiver and moan, and his eyes to glaze over as though he had viewed paradise. What did Mama do to Papa? Sazar carried the question with him as he tipped away.

Alex cradled Rose in his lap. He tickled her feet and played in her hair. Long after the water cooled, they sat cuddled together. She left the tub first. She dried herself then led Alex out of the water and toweled him off while he reveled in the fuss. Hand in hand, they retreated to their bedroom.

Seated at the vanity, he rubbed tonic into his hair and combed it carefully. While she laid his clothing on the bed, he stole at least one pinch from her behind. She kissed his shoulder and traded places with him.

Quickly, she brushed her hair in a bun, and stuck a pretty gold pin in it. Leaving a few tresses to kiss her face, she turned and winked at her husband, awaiting his approval.

He blew her a kiss then resumed buttoning his vest.

Before rising to get dressed, Rose paused to stare at Alex. Surely, she thought, I married the handsomest man in the world.

Sitting on the bed, she arched her foot and rolled a stocking up her leg. Humming softly, she stretched the other leg and did the same, and then attached the garters. After a deep breath, she sucked her stomach in, and hooked her corset. She exhaled, and donned her drawers and petticoat.

Leaning against the wardrobe, he observed his lovely wife. A lumped formed in his throat at the sight of her twirling before the mirror as free as a gypsy. The flared sleeves of the pretty orange calico dress flapped about her arms like wings. He went over, and massaged her neck. “You’re the only thing I never tire of.”

“That’s cause you’re away so much.”

“No. I just love my wife.”

“Sitting down to put on her shoes, she said, “Never matter the reason. It’s good to be loved, Papa. Heaven knows how I feel about you.”

He extended his hand and escorted her out to the hall. “Lil’ man,” he called.

Rose hurried off to prepare supper.

In the study, Alex found Sazar dusting the ships.

Neatly arranged on an étagère were exquisite watercraft replicas. The collection covered a spectrum of sizes and materials. Some were large, others small, and some in between. Many were fashioned from wood. Paper composed a few. Half a dozen were constructed of brass, five of leather, and one of glass.

Diligently, Sazar ran a cloth over a group of bottled ships bought in Haiti. Then he puckered his lips, and blew dust from a model cargo ship crafted of newspaper. Next came the task of dusting his favorite boat; one that Alex had purchased in Brazil. A twenty-seven inch, black leather schooner with a silver studded deck, a velvet rope, and a sterling anchor.

Laboring happily over the souvenirs and dreaming of his father's life at sea Sazar was fixed in a daze; completely unaware that Alex stood in the doorway looking on.

"Taking care of the beauties?"

"I take fine care of them while you're gone."

"I see." From a desk drawer, Alex retrieved a white handkerchief. He shook it out, and playfully ran it along some of the ships. Mockingly, he stared into the cloth, squinting to detect the faintest speckle. He shook his head in ridiculous disgust before throwing up his hands and slapping his thigh. "Do tell fella. Looks like our work here is done. Let's go to town."

Sazar burst into laughter and took a bow. "What will I get?"

"Whatever you fancy lil' man."

"My dear!" Alex called. "We're going out for a while."

"Don't be too long."

"We won't."

They returned at dusk. Coming up the walkway, they could smell Rose's cooking: candied yams, gumbo, cornbread, and lemon cake. Alex went to his study while Sazar eagerly trotted to the dining room, where Rose was setting the table.

"Mama! Mama! Look!" Next to the candlelight, he held out three marbles: a purple, a blue, and a black one"

Rose examined her son's treasures. "You and Papa find the most peculiar things."

"Swell huh?"

"They most certainly are son. Now put them away and go wash up."

"Yes ma'am."

Alex came in and seated himself. Proudly, he drank in Rose's splendor.

Wearing a lavender off-the-shoulder dress, she was dazzling. Oblong pearl earrings shimmered next to her radiant skin. She wore her hair in a single braid to one side, looped around an orchid. Her lips bore the stain of berry salve. She smiled seductively as she poured two glasses of sherry.

"I miss you when I'm gone. I miss you when I'm home."

"Well now, we two in a bushel. Have a drink."

Thank you, dolin'." Alex raised his glass in a toast.

Rose did the same and they drank.

Grinning, Sazar went to his mother and held out his hands. "All clean."

"I trust you honey." Rose filled a glass with cider and sat it before Sazar.

The three of them joined hands and bowed their heads.

Alex blessed the food. "Father, we thank you for this bread to strengthen and nourish our bodies. Lord, I thank you for keeping my family and myself; whether we're close together or far apart. Your grace abounds. Amen."

"Amen," agreed Rose and Sazar.

Running his finger along the cake, "Uhm . . . uhm," Alex smacked his lips.

"Behave." Rose giggled as she dished rice into Sazar's bowl.

"Mr. Sabatier's hosting a croquet game Saturday afternoon. Said he looks forward to seeing us. Will we go Papa?"

Alex pulled apart a piece of cornbread and sopped it in his gumbo. "This boy is hard to say no to."

"How could I know? I seldom deny Jorda men." Rose winked.

"Game's in the afternoon, so we can sleep late. Suits me fine. We'll go."

"Thanks Papa."

"By the way, how's Numa?"

"He's fine. His sister, Margenelle, is having another baby. They all thinks it's a boy cause she carrying it in her hips."

"They'll know for sure when it gets here. The Sabatiers are breeders. So far, boys and girls run neck and neck in that clan. I suppose that's good. Their name will never die."

"Ours won't either, Papa," Sazar said.

Rose passed Sazar a slice of cake. "You gon' give us a lot of fruit?"

"Yes, Mama."

"I admire your conviction," Alex said, wiping his mouth with a napkin. "Honey, I'm going out on the gallery, and smoke my pipe."

"I'll be out in a lil' while."

When Sazar finished his second helping of cake, he and Rose cleared the table. After the dishes were washed, she escorted him to his room. "Goodnight, love. Don't read too late. You had a full day."

"I won't, but the stars need watching."

"So do you." She kissed him on the cheek and left, closing the door behind her."

Sazar put on a nightshirt, and went to the telescope propped near the window. Through the lens he got a better look at a sky lit up with stars. He closed in on Polaris.

Save for the noise of crickets, the night was rather still.

Alex and Rose were outside courting like new lovers. They sat on the bench hugging, kissing, laughing, and talking. There they remained for over an hour. Just as Sazar started to yawn and ponder the moon's glow, they came inside.

Humming a lullaby, Rose went to their bedroom and brushed her hair. Before joining her, Alex rapped on Sazar's door. "Rest well son."

"You the same, Papa." Sazar said his prayers, turned down the mosquito net, and got into bed. Twice he almost drifted off, but fought sleep to listen for his parents' romance language. Blinking to stay awake, he waited. Shortly thereafter, the glare disappeared from the bottom of his door. He listened closely.

Their sheets rustled. Laughter. Out of kissing and panting evolved long drawn out sighs. They tossed. The mattress bounced; the bedstead rocked. Sparse groaning gave way to baritone whooping and extended alto cries.

He dozed off to the erotic chamber music that would play for the rest of summer; a blissful season except for one grave intrusion.

In July, Sazar fell ill with yellow fever; which tended to plague New Orleans during summer. Within a day he was consumed by a high temperature and too feeble to walk. Then he became delirious and jaundiced; coughing up black puke followed.

Four loving hands nursed him. Well meaning neighbors brought remedies that they swore by. After sniffing the concoctions, Alex decided that most were too foul to pour into his son. Nevertheless, he thanked them graciously. As soon as they left, to the privy the potions went. Hospitals could do precious little for those stricken with the fever. Besides, Alex wanted Sazar at home. After watching his son suffer for three days and fearful that his condition might worsen, Alex decided to visit Madame Curry's garden.

Thick and blooming with blue and white flowers, wisteria entangled the black cast-iron fence that surrounded the stately ocean blue raised Italianate villa on St. Ann. Redolent bouquets of lavender, honeysuckle, and jasmine lined the walk and played paradise to butterflies and bees. Draped in Spanish moss, a grand old magnolia tree held sway among the dogwoods, and shaded a cherub fountain inhabited by gold fish and water lilies.

Alex stepped onto the gallery, ducking under one of five mature resurrection ferns, only to have the tendrils of string beans dust his shoulder. Before a host of clay pots containing ivies, cacti, pink impatiens, red geraniums, and peonies, he knocked on the door. No one answered. Careful not to drop the burlap sack folded under his arm, he snapped a couple of freshly picked cherries from a basket then knocked again; still no answer. Following a trail of vibrant purple wandering jew, he went to the backyard where the fruit trees and vegetable gardens were.

On a small tract of land separated by a short wooden fence, grew full bunches of collard and mustard greens, sweet red peppers, large cabbages, and ripe juicy tomatoes.

Navigating through a triangle of trees, he stepped on some blueberries. He dragged his foot along the grass, and kept walking. A flowering banana palm engaged in a subtle fan dance caressed his face with its wide smooth leaves and poked its firm green fruit at his elbow. He had barely passed the cherry tree when the scent of lemons circled him.

Olives fell into a jar stationed next to a ladder. Several rungs above, a spry matronly figure under a floppy straw hat delved among the branches humming softly.

"Good evening, Madame Curry."

"Alex! Is that you?" She climbed down. "Well, hello there." A welcoming smile stretched across her kind ebony face that glistened from the heat.

"You're looking well my dear."

"You the same, son. Uhm . . . your boy still sick?"

"Oui, Madame."

"You need to break the fever. Help yourself."

Alex walked over to the chinaberry tree that sat off to itself. Pretty but poisonous, the leaves had been used medicinally for as long as anybody could remember. Expeditiously, he shook out his sack and filled it with leaves. When he finished, he tossed the load over his shoulders, and waved good-bye. "Merci, Madame."

"Anytime. I'll keep you in my prayers."

At sunset Rose sponged Sazar off then Alex covered his son's naked body with leaves. The three of them held hands. Humbled by reverence, sincerity, and desperation, Alex prayed. "Father, you heal the sick and raise the dead. I'm asking you, in the holy name of Jesus Christ of Nazareth, to cast this infirmity out of our son. Lord bless him with good health and the fullness of days. Thy will be done. Amen."

"Amen," Rose said.

Sazar fell asleep within minutes. Exhausted, Rose and Alex retired in their day clothes. She slept in a bedside chair while he dozed off in bed with Sazar. Throughout the night they would take turns checking their son's breathing, and once give him water for thirst.

Morning inaugurated to the chirping of sparrows. The fog dissipated gradually, unveiling a clear but very hot day. A palmetto palm brushed against the shutters, awakening Alex. Halfheartedly, he yawned and stretched before touching sleeping Sazar's forehead. The fever was gone. He plucked a leaf, and effortlessly it crumbled between his fingers. With gentle, sweeping, heedful motions he brushed the leaves off of Sazar, and kissed his mouth. "Thank you Lord." Alex glanced at a still sleeping Rose, fluffed his pillow, and returned to rest. Unaware that his seed would make it to manhood without so much as the common cold.

September. It was cool outdoors. Good play weather. Sazar sat on the steps awaiting his parents, wishing that he could go to Lake Pontchartrain with Numa, instead of seeing his father off. Good-byes were usually difficult and lengthy for Rose. Alex was going offshore for over two months, and scheduled to return on November 13th, the day after Sazar's birthday.

Careful not to scuff his shoes, Sazar stepped on a few unsuspecting ladybugs.

Rose came outside. Her face was tense. "Papa's almost ready," she said curtly.

"I'm not."

"Me neither, honey." She licked her finger, stooped down, and smoothed his hair.

Alex came out and sat his bags down. "Y'all 'bout ready?" he asked, fitting on his cap.

"I suppose." Rose answered, throwing her arms around his waist.

"You make it hard for me to go."

"Harder still for me to let go."

"Dolin', you married a sailor." He raised her chin, and looked into her eyes. "Remember my heart is always with you."

Missing him before he was gone, she fell into a brand new embrace. Her tears dampened his shirt. He coddled her face and with his handkerchief he dried her tears. "Girl, when I come home," he searched her face for a trace of peace, "it's gon' be like carnival for you and me."

In spite of a twitching lip, Rose forced a smile. "Alright Papa."

Sazar stood up, dusted off his rump, and picked up the smaller of his father's bags.

"You ready lil' man?"

"Yes Papa!" Sazar pinched Rose's arm. "Come on Mama, don't cry."

The Mississippi River and the city in its elbow clove inextricably. The river brought the world to New Orleans and New Orleans to the world. By river the Crescent City became a village of mingled peoples. Sugar, rice, cotton, and tobacco were New Orleans' harvests and staples of prosperity that were exported by way of the Mississippi. Trouble too came by river: war, floods, and pestilence. In spite of all that, the river blessed the city.

Upon entering the port, fortune seekers could ask for no greater inspiration than the spectacle along the river. Palatial plantation homes with Greek columns and grand verandas graced the frontage. Legions of ships lined the levee, mostly steamboats, puffing clouds of thick black smoke into the air.

In the midst of it all, the Jordas were separated by a hedge of love. Alex knelt down and hugged Sazar. "I love you, son."

"I love you, Papa"

"You take that girl for me."

"I will. Have a sweet sail."

Alex stood and placed his hand across his heart. "Hold me close."

"In deeds, thoughts, and prayers."

"What more could a father ask?"

"Til next time lil' man," Alex pinched Sazar's cheek, and beckoned Rose to his arms. He stroked her hair and kissed her. "Tell me you gon' be alright?"

With her voice cracking, she answered, "I'll get along, but I won't be alright til you get home."

"Good enough, lady." He squeezed her tightly.

Knowing that a comfortable time to let go would never present itself, they withdrew simultaneously. Alex took his bags and went up the dock. He zigzagged from side to side, dodging stevedores as they hauled bales of cotton and large crates.

Rose and Sazar looked on from the wharf. Customarily, Alex would wave at them from the main deck until the ship sailed so far upriver that they appeared as blank faces among the masses.

He boarded the merchant ship Evangeline, went onto the main deck, and waved wholeheartedly. Happily, Sazar did the same; Rose waved sacrificially. After the crew drew the anchor in and the ship gradually floated away from the levee, Alex blew them a kiss and waved once more. Then he turned, faced the sail, and never looked back.

His actions struck his family as strange, but affected each of them differently. Sazar felt a tinge of confusion. Rose, on the other hand, felt the earth breaking beneath her feet. She took a few moments to steady her wracked emotions, so that she could speak. "Let's go." She latched on to Sazar's hand.

After being dragged a short distance, he let go. She stopped. Maybe he is getting too big to hold his mama's hand, she thought. They continued along the riverfront with Sazar lagging behind.

They visited the French Market. Too agitated to browse or bargain, Rose bought from the first vendor she saw, who happened to be stationed near the entrance. Quickly, she filled her basket with pomegranates, apples, okra, tomatoes, and a jar of apricot preserves. She paid for the items, gave the change to Sazar, and waited while he went to purchase sugarcane.

As swiftly as they came—they went. This time Sazar kept up with Rose without holding her hand. They wandered through Jackson Square. Strutting with her head high enough to succumb to vertigo, Rose bumped into an old Haitian man. "Pardon me, sir." Embarrassed and startled, she stepped back to catch her breath. "I didn't see you."

"In a hurry, lady?" The old man sat on a blanket next to his wares. An open suitcase lay on a rickety table; under which a folded potato sack supported one of the legs that had rotted to splinters. He sold charms, amulets, bracelets, earrings, and colorful sorts of beads.

Rose browsed while Sazar waited aside.

"Trinkets for the heart, charms for the soul." The old man spoke just loud enough for Rose to hear him. He heavy words stretched out like a long desolate journey. The folds of time had creased his serene sable face. Time, elements, and debris had yellowed his white kinky hair. "Pour femme jolie, Sinclair give good price," he said, stirring his fingers through the tray of beads beside him.

Though she found his voice hauntingly familiar, she could not place it right then. Suddenly, her son crossed her mind. She looked around to find him waiting patiently. At ease, her attention returned to the jewelry. A jumble of pendants: crosses, saints, coins, and zodiacs. She handled a few; held them up for a closer look. Buried under the ones she moved was a sterling crux with a pair of wings on its crossbar.

She began to cry.

Sazar rushed to her side. "Mama, what's wrong?"

"I miss Papa so."

He followed her gaze, and recognized the pendant as identical to the one that his father wore, and had worn for as long as he could recall. "Please don't cry. Let's go home." He hugged her waist.

"Alright." She dried her eyes, dropped fifty cents in the till, took the crux, and went home.

Trying not to sob again, Rose hung her shawl and purse on the hall-tree then went to the kitchen. Sazar followed. He sat in a chair across from the stove, sucking sugarcane while she stored food. She shuffled items around the pantry the way a madwoman would stir a pot.

Usually she fell into a mourning period during the initial days of Alex's absence. However, Sazar had never seen her so despondent. He figured on what to say to her, but could think of nothing that might comfort her. Since he couldn't take another crying spell, he retreated to his room.

After washing his face and hands, he withdrew to the gallery with a sack of marbles.

Down on all fours, he set his mark, and shot balls under the bench, against the door, and into the yard. Occasionally, he greeted neighbors; otherwise, his concentration was set on play. His heart, however, was with his mother.

The first letter from Alex was supposed to arrive in about two weeks. Depending on the efficiency of the postal system, subsequent letters would arrive biweekly or triweekly. Alex and Rose had agreed on that schedule when they met. Sazar counted on the letter to calm his mother and restore joy to their household. Resting his cheek on his left hand, he squinted and thumped a big pink marble into the grass.

Propelled by high autumn winds, the swag billowed over the canopy. Sazar awoke, rolled over on his naked back, and faced a window that shared morning and breezes that tickled his skin. He blew slumber out of his lungs and inhaled the cool new air. Having underwent a summer growth spurt, stretching his arms and legs felt awkward because he had not yet adjusted to his lengthened torso. Maybe I'll catch a frog today, he thought. Spurred on by ambition, he jumped out of bed, got down on his knees, bowed his head, and prayed. "Our father which art in heaven, hallowed be thy name. Thy kingdom come. Thy will be done, as in heaven, so in earth. Give us day by day our daily bread. And forgive us our sins; for we also forgive—"

Rose knocked on the door then looked inside. "Your father is in—" She fell silent.

Clenching the letter, she stepped back behind the door. Yet she could not take her eyes off Sazar. His beauty reminded her of just how much he had taken after his father. The graceful length of his neck, the still developing strong back, and beautifully defined limbs. He had inherited Alex's coloring; the only difference was the hint of fire in his flesh imparted by her. Like hers, his eyes were dark. The first time she held him, she had hoped he was as rich on the inside as he was on the outside.

"Every one that is indebted to us. And lead us not into temptation; but deliver us from evil. Amen." Sazar opened his eyes and stood. "Come in, Mama."

Waving the letter, Rose said, "Your father is in Arkansas." Smiling from ear to ear, she read further down. "He's going to buy your birthday present in the West Virginia."

"Well Mama, that's swell. Papa's fine."

"Yes, he is."

"So are we."

"Vrai." Rose folded the note and left.

The first letter brought Rose some calm. As did the letter that arrived on October 10, which Alex had written while he was in West Virginia. But she still wasn't altogether at peace. Hence, Rose's behavior changed radically when the third letter did not come by the end of October. Of course the post office sometimes experienced grave delays. A few times Alex had arrived in New Orleans before his final letters did. Also his ship might dock a day or so earlier or later. He was scheduled to come home in two weeks. Nevertheless, Rose was on edge, and left to cling to the correspondence she had.

During the coming days, Sazar would seldom see her without the letters. She read them coming and going; in the middle of housework, as she sat at her vanity, when she awoke in the morning, and before falling asleep at night. Repeatedly, she studied the notes as though she might derive some clue or revelation that she had overlooked in prior readings.

Sazar figured she must have poured over them in his absence. Gradually, she began to handle the letters differently. The way a survivor handles the ashes of the dead. With great reverence, much care, and some fear. She prayed incessantly, and wore her rosary all the time. This seemed to keep her stable—stably fretting over Alex. Her altered state made Sazar wonder if her frayed nerves might snap.

One evening, after playing with Numa, Sazar came home to silence and darkness. He had not seen his mother since before he left for school. Tired and hungry, he took off his vest and shoes and left them in the drawing room. He went to the kitchen and found his supper on the stove. He peeled the waxed paper back from a plate of baked chicken and steamed squash then poured himself a glass of cider.

On the way to his room he saw light coming from his parents' bedroom.

Standing just beyond the threshold, he viewed Rose sitting beside her wedding chest. She held a small pearl encrusted box. In it was a lock of Alex's hair. She coddled the hair between her fingers, passed it under her nose then folded the recent letter around it, and placed that note on top of a stack of eight years worth of letters arranged in chronological order. She closed the chest and rested her cheek on it.

Helplessly, he watched his mother sink in grief. Why she so sad? he wondered. He wanted to say something. But what? Hello? Goodnight? I love you? The words would not funnel out of his throat. So he went to his room and ate alone.

Rose became ever more detached as the date of Alex's homecoming neared. She and Sazar saw each other at brief intervals. After school and Mass, he ran off with his friends. He left his clothing scattered all over the house. Rose failed to remind him of chores or see that he ate meals; thus, he bought plenty to nibble on in the streets. He gorged on candy, pickles, cakes, and fried meats. Though he wasn't hiding from his mother, he was definitely steering clear of her pain; and she stayed too preoccupied to draw him back in.

One Saturday, Sazar and his pals pooled their monies to purchase a jug of spirits. The next morning he was hungover and unable to attend Mass. Rose made little attempt to diagnose him; but his puke bore the odor and stain of his temptation—cheap ruby wine. She gave him broth and mint tea, and cleaned his mess. Monday morning, like a nurse arriving at the hospital to discover that her patient had recuperated, Rose went to Sazar's room to find that he had gone to school.

November 12, Sazar's eighth birthday, came and went quietly. Rose baked him coconut cake, and raised his weekly allowance to seventy-five cents. They spent the evening together eating double portions of cake and reading the *Picayune.* At least on that day, he moved back into his mother's radius. Not that he was completely comfortable with her; actually, her vibe had begun to wear on him. On the eve of his father's anticipated return, fear crept upon Sazar.

Before he lay down to sleep, he had but one supplication, "Lord, please bring Papa home." In his dark room, he lay in bed staring up at the ivory swag, which he ordained his dream-catcher. His mind roamed to a bastion of yesterdays. Vividly, he recalled how he and his parents had journeyed to and from the port of New Orleans so many times before. Out of pure hope, he tried to envision that picture for tomorrow, but to no avail. Next he strove to summons a chimera of his parents making love. All he managed to produce were two lumps of clay lying in a pool of water. Suddenly, the whole notion felt like sin—sick sin. Frustrated by his stagnant imagination, he decided to test his memory for sound. Unmistakably, the rich baritone voice resonated paternal and profound. *I love you lil' man.* Safe. He rolled over, and looked forward to sleep.

Rose leaned against the barrier with her arms folded, holding her shoulders stiff against the cold.

From the distance she saw the Evangeline creeping into port. It was the kind of ship that artist pained to capture on canvas: a multi-masted dark vessel with ivory sails, and a lion figurehead. Steamboats that had lagged behind it, peddled ahead.

Finally, the Evangeline reached the basin.

"There it is," Rose said.

Sazar stood on his toes. He liked to see the rudder cutting toward the harbor.

When the ship was anchored, the captain waved from the helm. Crewmen who were free to go did so. They departed in groups and pairs. But Alex, who was usually one of the first off the ship, was not among them.

Stevedores started unloading the cargo deck.

Anxiously, Rose and Sazar looked on.

Then a man who was familiar swaggered down the ramp. His bushy mustache shifted as his lip twitched from side to side. Winter had banished the glow from his bronze skin, and left it ashen. A powerful physique and worldly charm afforded him a commanding presence. Squinting his hazel eyes at the horizon, he hesitated and accounted for all of his bags; then Joseph Anthony stepped forward. He spotted Rose. It helped that she and Sazar were standing where they always did; though her double-bladed stare would have led him to her anyway.

Still, overcome with apprehension, he could not yet look her in the eye.

Joseph treaded through the crowds. He tightened his grip on the bags, and squeezed between two longshoreman hauling cotton bales.

Frantically, Rose tried to flag him down. She took Sazar's hand, and moved through pockets of idlers. Though a myriad of faces marred their lines of sight, she and Joseph saw each other in flashes.

Rising to the challenge of keeping up, Sazar stepped on his mother's heels here and there. The sweat of her desperation made his palm slick. After much crisscrossing, they were face to face with Joseph.

The pitiful silence between Mr. Anthony and Rose made Sazar wish he were grown.

She looked down at the bags that Joseph rested near her feet, Alex's bags.

She willed herself to speak. Bluntly, she asked, "Where is Alex?"

A grief-laden expression claimed Joseph's face. His eyes fell to the ground then to Sazar, and inevitably back to Rose. He placed his hands on her shoulders. "Please, my dear, not in front of—"

Violently, she broke away form his grasp. "He wants to know, just like I do!" Aware that she drew attention to herself, she lowered her voice. "Tell me now."

Joseph took off his cap and fumbled it between his hands. Once, twice, and a third time his lips parted; yet the words refused to come forth.

Distress clamped his tongue. Hastened by her angst, and what little courage he could muster, Joseph settled himself to speak. "Rose, we . . . docked in Mississippi, Port Gibson. Me and Alex took a room in town. On our last night there, we went to a saloon. Whole lot of folks be there. We sat a long spell, drankin' with some of the crew. We down plenty whiskey. Fore long we danced a fella's share with the ladies. They was dancin' gals. So then we sit a spell more, and drank another round. While the other fellas carry on with them gals. Fore long, I had to relieve myself. So I tell Alex, I be right back. I go on outside. When I get back, I don't see Alex at the table. So I look around, he not at the bar. So I ask the fellas—they don't know! Now, I was just about drunk, but I still sees all the same gals that was there fore I left. So I knows he wasn't with none of them. I get scared cause me and Alex always let each other know where we going, what we gon' do. Then I think maybe he get tired, and went on back to the room." Joseph held his cap to his chest, and sighed.

"So I tells the others that I'm heading to the boardinghouse to see if Alex is there. He wasn't there," his voice began to crack, "but his belongings was. I go on back to the saloon, reckoning he might've made it back. I drank a few more shots. Lil' later, I go back to the room. With everything in me, I hoped to see Alex in the room safe. But no! I lay across the cot, waiting. Never did shut my eyes. Next morning, we boarded ship. No Alex."

A wall of despair enclosed Rose and Sazar; not even the rally of public commotion could penetrate it. Astounded and helpless, they stood stoically before Joseph Anthony for a chronic minute. Then, Alex's elegy sank in, and they wept openly.

When Joseph hurriedly shoved his cap inside his coat, he remembered Alex's wages. Lacing his voice with optimism, he said, "Here girl." He gave Rose an envelope. "Captain give me Alex pay. Ought to be plenty for you to get by on, for a while anyway. Til you find work and all."

Dazedly, she surveyed her husband's legacy. Her inheritance: his pay, his baggage, and his son. She wiped her face with on coat-sleeve, held her head up, and straightened her shoulders. Sazar had calmed down; she needed to be strong for him.

If Joseph's twitching mouth was any indication of *the shakes,* then he sorely craved a drink. He glanced around nonchalantly, trying to avoid looking Sazar in the face. Though he was well aware that the boy watched his every frazzled move.

Sazar took it upon himself to make Joseph's departure less burdensome. He seized one of his father's bags, and stared Joseph down until he got his attention. "Good-bye, Mr. Anthony."

"God bless y'all," Joseph mumbled.

"Mama, let's go."

They meandered home. Devastating, irrevocable realities unwound and pressed upon Rose. She was left alone to raise her son. Without a grave, she had no place to honor Alex, nor anyplace to vent. Without a body, she had no assurance whether she grieved a dead man or a living one. In baby steps, she began the process of reconciling with her bittersweet harvest: a ghost and a bloodline. She had one legacy to mourn and another to foster.

Sixteen months later, they still survived on savings. The cottage was almost paid for, and they lacked nothing; except Alex. At times Alex was everything. Nevertheless, they thrust themselves into their routines.

Tasks became partitions between sanity and madness. Rose cooked, cleaned, shopped, and cared for her garden. She refused to participate in any of the ladies' auxiliaries at St. Augustine Church, nor did she accept invitations to any social gatherings. She and Miss Irene were as close as ever; otherwise, Rose operated solo.

Sazar excelled in school, especially literature and philosophy. He did his chores without having to be reminded. Every now and then he played away from home until just before dark, which upset Rose a little but she didn't make much of a fuss. After all, he was a boy, and boys were apt to wander. He abandoned the marbles altogether, and never opened the bag of agate ones—his final gift from Alex. Whereas he still dusted the ships, the twinkle had long gone from his eyes.

Many evenings while Rose sat in the parlor crocheting into the wee hours of the night, Sazar studied and kept her company. After finishing his lessons, he would read to her; which always seemed to lighten her mood. As she looped the needle through the yarn, concentrating on the pattern, she listened to his lively recitations. During such times, Rose, in spite of herself, smiled out of pure joy.

On a warm day in March, Rose and Sazar had been shopping in the quarter. They walked down Marais, a few blocks from home.

Above them, a flock of seagulls formed a circle and squealed riotously. They looked up at the birds. Suddenly, their strident cries ceased. The birds flapped their wings in unison, and flew off on one accord, migrating to some other waterfront paradise. Now the Jordas minded the path ahead again. Secretly, they too longed to fly.

Nodding at neighbors here and there, they walked in silence. They were just about home, when Rose felt someone staring at her from behind; not the voracious stare of a man, but the probing consideration of a woman. She glanced from right to left, hoping to view the spectator peripherally. No luck. So she quickened her pace; as did Sazar.

Her apt response compelled the observer to approach her, for fear of missing the opportunity. "Hello there, Miss Rose."

Rose stopped and turned around. "Good day, Viola."

That was all anybody ever called her—Viola. A homely brown-skinned woman. She wore thick pompadour-style wigs; she owned an array of colors: red, black, brown, ash. Today she wore the black one. She had relatives in the Tremé, among them her aging mother. So she was not a complete stranger to Rose. Viola's reputation, however, was known all over New Orleans. She was rumored to run a house of ill repute.

News of Alex's disappearance came to her via front porch gossip. She knew that Rose had never labored away from home, and that she had not taken any suitors. In fact, she openly spurned male advances. Viola calculated that Rose would soon need one of two things: a new husband or work. A careful review of her delicate beauty and feminine grace left Viola hard-pressed to believe that Alex had deserted her by choice. Anyway, many men would pay top dollar for a temporary stay.

Embarrassed that a woman of questionable character had approached her in the middle of the street, on a Saturday, at high noon, under her circumstances, Rose gave her basket to Sazar. "Here, I'll be on directly."

Because he was curious about the woman with the surly voice, he deliberately walked slowly.

"Go on home. I'm right behind you."

He obeyed.

Before Rose knew what to say, she found herself reaching for the card that Viola extended. It read: Viola Latson *The Jade* 33 South Basin Street.

"Summer bound to be some kind of hot," Viola said, twirling a pink parasol that matched her dress.

"Yes it is."

"That's a fine looking boy you got there."

"Thank you." Worried that people might be staring at her, Rose looked around nervously. But folks were going about their own business. "I have to get home."

"I understand. You take care."

They parted. One headed east to home; the other went to visit.

For the next month or so, whenever they saw each other, they were cordial. Not once did Viola imply that Rose was in need, nor did she inquire about her plans. Viola refrained from boasting about how much money could be made in so little time; neither did she promote the *purple arts.* She never alluded to her profession at all. And she kept her interest in Rose off the grapevine. For Viola was wise to one infallible truth: nothing fosters an open mind like desperation.

Rose stood before her bedroom window with her nightgown rolled up to her breasts. Winds were neither savage nor mild. Cool breezes rippled over her thighs and whispered in her navel. She breathed, delaying the in and out breaths. She closed her eyes, and let her fingers prance over her stomach and roam her private hair. Every whiff of air purged her spirit of something old; peace was ripe for the picking.

A strong gust of wind rustled the trees while a hooting owl traded one branch for another. During the interlude, hope seeped into Rose's heart. For the first time in a long time, she felt whole.

Slowly, a trowel of clarity excavated the catacombs of her psyche. Now her deepest concerns formed a procession. One by one, they approached the throne of her consciousness to plead their cases.

Money was thinning out. She did not want another husband—now nor ever. She would be damned if she worked in white folks houses; she hated them. Alex was gone, but all of their dreams did not go with him. She still wanted Sazar to go to college. She had to do something soon. Captured and calmed by the tranquil night, she moved closer to the window, freeing her gown to fall to her ankles. She unbraided her hair, shook it loose, and ran her hands through it. Far from sleepy, she sat in the window seat. In the sphere of sound thinking, one truth prevailed: she and Sazar were all alone.

Both she and Alex came from splintered relations.

Alex's father and namesake was a drunken carpenter, now eking out a living in Houma. Marie, Alex's mother, had been a transient figure who passed in and out of his life until he left home.

As Rose's thoughts drifted to her own family, her jaws tightened, webs formed at the corners of her eyes. Here she had to be careful. Rage had blood, bones, and a pulse all its own. So she let it rest for the time being. Instead she chose to let a swaying palm soothe her. She found it intriguing how she noticed things under the moonlight that she would have missed in broad daylight. Things likc thc caterpillar scooting across the olive jar, a petal forsaking its daisy, a cat scratching the trunk of a tree. She rested her head on the window frame, and hugged her knees. Then without invitation, her history played.

Her mother, Ruth died in labor when Rose was five years old. Ruth was gentle natured, fragile, and wanting for love. So she married the first man that talked soft to her.

Ezra, Rose's father, was a *sweet man*; he went from one woman to the next, living off them. Some he stayed with for a long time, like Ruth. Others he stuck around long enough to ruin. If he had not left behind a trail of children, he would have left nothing at all. The only thing that Ezra liked less than commitment was work. He and Ruth lived on a plot of her parents' land. A plot that Ruth mostly worked by herself. He was always fixin' to do something. Fixin' to feed the hogs, fixin' to separate the chickens, or fixin' to gather eggs. There was one thing, however, that he did without any proclamation. As Ruth labored in the throes of death with his baby mortifying in her womb, Ezra patted Rose on the head, and abandoned them.

Matthew LaPomeret had been much more than a grandfather. From him Rose learned to read, to dance, and to hope. But pneumonia took him before her ninth birthday. After that, she and her grandmother, Adele, were left together. Whereas her grandmother provided for her, Adele was not maternal. When she wasn't working the farm, she was drinking moonshine or entertaining younger men. She only saw Sazar once when he was an infant. She said that she was glad that he was fair-skinned like Alex. Not long after her visit, Adele died on her front porch, clutching a damn near empty whiskey jug.

Now Rose grew tired. The air began to chill her. Her only cover—a quilt of bitter patches which she would rather have burned. As she pulled the shutters in, the final zephyr blew in the spirit of sacrifice. Sure enough, it anchored itself amidst love and conviction.

What was a tainted morality for the one person in the world that she had left to love?

A Chinese foo dog's roaring mouth piqued Rose's interest. She reached to the right and touched the pointed teeth. Suspended in a leap, the enchanting white marble beast and its twin guarded the Jade, and incited Rose to know what lay within its walls. She stood on her toes and peered through the small oval window, but the stained glass played secret-keeper. Carefully but eagerly, she pressed the scroll knocker to the door.

Viola answered. "Hello there." A yellow and white dress with a high lace collar softened her presence. The ash wig and a little rouge on her cheeks made her pleasing.

"Good afternoon." Rose tried hard to conceal her fascination as she entered the foyer. The truth was—she was stunned.

Emerald-colored wallpaper with embossed velvet fleur-de-lis made entering the bordello feel like stepping into a jcwcl box. Atop a black floral marquetry console table, jasmine incense burned from a brass pagoda. A watercolor of a female torso hung above.

Viola led Rose into the parlor where there was more to feast her eyes on: a three-tier chandelier in a cascade of lime-green crystals, a sprawling carpet in a pattern of Siamese dancers. An ivory brocade swag adorned the bay window that gave light to a full-grown datura, blooming bell shaped yellow-orange flowers.

After Viola seated Rose on a serpentine back sofa covered in a mélange of pretty cushions, she sat across from her in a green velvet armchair. While Rose absorbed the mystical atmosphere, Viola sized her up again. In doing so, she caught a puzzled expression unfolding on the visitor's lovely face. "It's still early."

"Oh!" Rose said, blushing.

Both of them laughed from their guts.

For the first time ever, Viola saw Rose smile unbridled and unprompted. A thousand candles lit at once could not rival her light.

When Rose caught her breath, her shoulders dropped, and she relaxed comfortably on the sofa. Now she was at home in a house that she once feared, and with a woman who used to make her nervous.

A pretty young dark girl entered the parlor. She wore an apron, and a pressed red handkerchief covered her hair. She filled two cups with tea and gave one to Viola. "You take sugar and milk, ma'am?" she asked Rose.

"Just sugar. Thank you."

She served and left.

"I been thinking about working for you, but I can't live here. You know, I have Sazar."

"Of course. I have nine girls; four of them live off premises."

"I can't work everyday."

"Dear," Viola smiled, "no one can."

"What I mean . . . I can't work as much as your other girls."

"How about three, maybe four nights a week?"

"That'll do fine."

"Good."

"Oh!" Rose sipped some tea. Nervously, she bowed her head and nibbled the inside of her lip. "See . . . the only man I ever known was Alex."

Viola sat her cup down, went to sit beside Rose, and held her hand. "This is nothing like being with your husband. What you do with these men is just business. And it don't last long either. They get strictly what they pay for."

"But they pay us to—"

"They pay for relief."

"When relief comes in a pretty package, they pay more."

Usually, Rose worked for Viola three times a week; sometimes four. She would leave home at sundown and return before the break of dawn. She earned ample money to support herself and Sazar while steadily adding to a savings account. Work did not interfere with domesticity. She cooked three meals a day, did laundry on Mondays, and kept floors clean enough to eat off.

The best part was that she and Sazar grew closer, and their time spent together grew all the richer. As she helped him with homework, or during meals, or while they did the dishes, he disclosed the details of his day and the matters of his heart. He revealed a deep consciousness regarding religion, morality, race, and his future. Far as Rose could tell, he was becoming a young man of substance, and he made his mama feel ten feet tall.

With her house in order, she had but one remaining foe, her conscience. Slowly, she brought it under submission by letting it alone. Formulating a lie to tell Sazar about her employment was a different issue. Fully aware that he was too worldly to be wholly deceived; she, nevertheless, wanted some kind of shroud on hand. Inevitably, the time came. When it did, he caught her off guard.

Rose had worked at the Jade for about a month. One evening, she sat at her vanity, pinning her hair. Seeing the door to her room wide open, Sazar ventured in. At first he stood next to her quietly as she groomed herself. She winked at him. When he moved to lean on the footboard, their reflections shared the mirror. Their eyes locked.

"What's on your mind handsome?"

Sazar curled his bottom lip, and wrinkled his forehead. "What all you do at the boarding house?"

"Cher, I told you—I clean rooms." Rose's hands fell to her lap. Shocked, but she didn't let it show. So she decided not to build a raft to help a sinking lie float after all. She turned around. One look. *I am the parent; you are the child.*

"Yes ma'am." He looked on as she finished her hair. He knew good and well that women who looked like her seldom cleaned rooms; and if they did, they didn't style their hair in fancy upsweeps, wear pretty gowns, bathe in sweet-smelling potions, paint their faces, or rub toilet water into their skins.

There she sat, gorgeous in a magenta silk dress with bell sleeves and a ruffled heart neckline. She slid earrings into her ears then held a strand of pearls to her neck.

He went over and clasped her necklace for her.

"Give Mama some sugar."

"I love you, Mama. Be careful."

"I love you. Goodnight."

Spring of 1877 was the season of Sazar's maturity. He was set to graduate from secondary school with distinction, and scheduled to begin studies at Straight University in the fall. Since he kept his marks high, Rose allowed him to serve as a metalsmith apprentice for a colored jeweler. He even crafted a few pieces for her. Just as he learned to melt, blast, mold, and sculpt silver and gold, life itself fashioned and refined him.

At sixteen, he inherited his father's full-blown likeness. Exquisite jaw line, broad shoulders, fine build, and all. He was somewhat reserved and a little serious. He and Numa Sabatier were still as close as brothers. Sazar was adored by his teachers.

He got along alright with most of his classmates, but he never backed down from a brawl; by bloodshed he reformed the school bully. As far as courting was concerned, his was a Casanova spirit.

Whenever he read in class, overcome with butterflies, girls wiggled in their seats and batted their eyes. He courted a handful of belles; each desirable in her own way. Camille was tall like him, and a great dancer. Vita's hips were wide, and she beat him at chess. Babet had tight blonde curls and a mole on her lip. Cute Poupon had a dimple in her chin, and spoke the Queen's English. After school, he usually walked one of them home. Picnics on the lake and ice cream dates were reserved for the weekends. Like clockwork, Sazar's dates typically culminated with a budding beauty wrestling him down behind an outhouse, in a flowerbed, or in the shadow of some imposing tomb in St. Louis No.1 for mad kissing and feverish petting. A few were bold enough to explore him in the unchaperoned parlors of their homes. Yet as much as he enjoyed female company, none of them came close to winning his heart. Women, both young and old, never seemed to tire of studying him, so he studied himself; mostly his inner man.

Lampposts and a full pearly moon were guiding lights as Sazar and Numa frolicked through the Vieux Carré. It was Saturday night, and they were celebrating Numa's poker victory. The two of them took turns swigging on a bottle of whiskey. A few blocks behind they had discarded the strong

Cuban cigars that made their throats itch and had them coughing like babes.

"Jorda, I'm tellin' you, one day, I'm gon' be the richest hustler in all of Nawlins'. Gon' buy me a steamboat and race it. And one of them big houses cross the river in Algiers got my name on it. Mark my word."

"Good luck brother. It's gon' take a lot more than twenty dollars to do all that."

"Alright, Mister Straight and Narrow. I suppose you plan to conquer the world with your law."

"Commercial law."

"Pardon me."

"My friend, I wish you well; but you got your way and I got mine. Anyhow, you could do a lot more than gamble."

"Look—my hands not steady enough to set no rubies and pearls. I sure can't sit and read for hours on end like you."

"You used to love horses, you could breed. And your old man taught you everything he know about cabinetmaking."

"Yeah, but working the family business with my puritan brothers—hah! I rather live in the swamps."

They took Conti to cross onto Basin. They stumbled upon a stretch of bawdy houses. Like bloodshot crystal balls, red lanterns lit every porch. Half-naked hussies hung out of windows and loitered in doorways yelling propositions. Very few passed for attractive. Far too many were missing teeth that were undoubtedly lost in brawls. Wearing patches over gouged eyes, several of them looked like pirates. Skinny poverty-stricken girls looked as lost as lambs; they had sold their virtue to ward off starvation. Grey haired women's sullen wrinkled faces mapped their hardships.

Numa and Sazar walked about three blocks when they neared houses that had brick steps and nice paint. The doors were closed and no one was shouting from these establishments. These were *sweet houses.* The women were good-looking and the patrons had to be fully dressed (wearing a shirt and shoes).

Toward the end of the row there was a two-story house with a pretty "iron lace" balcony. As they passed the house, a comely girl with skin the color of wet sand and a bushy brown ponytail that tickled her fanny stormed onto the balcony weeping hysterically. She stood off in corner, and buried her face in her hands. Her sobs were heavy and sickening; the kind that led to swollen eyes, stomach and head aches.

"She something, ain't she?" Numa said.

"Yeah . . . she is. Wonder what she crying about?"

"Anything. Women like her got enough to be sad about."

Another woman came out to comfort her. She moved too quickly for Sazar and Numa to really see her face. In seconds, she had her back to them. But judging from her delicate profile, coiffured jet hair, petite form clad in a lace grey dress, and the confidence with which she moved, they suspected that she was a stunning woman and somewhat older that the one she consoled.

The lady in grey stroked the crying girl's face, and caught the flow of her tears with a handkerchief. The girl calmed down eventually. She attempted to smile, but the hurt would not let her. Gratitude was in her eyes though. When the women felt the presence of stares, they became uneasy. So naturally they searched for their audience. Below they found a pair of inquisitive onlookers. Both women's attention fell to Sazar.

Although he was certainly attracted to the younger woman, the other woman concerned him. Deeply. Personally.

A tinge of shame caused the lady in grey to turn away briefly. Then a stroke of boldness swept over her, and she faced Sazar.

There is a valley of difference between knowing the truth and seeing the truth. So there they were, saying nothing but communicating profoundly.

If Sazar had moved, he would have fallen to his knees. It hit him. It hit him hard that his mother's love was a wide green pasture without a fence. He marveled at what she was made of. What God had given his father in courage and physical stamina, surely he had endowed his mother tenfold with fortitude.

Rose waved.

Sazar waved back. Then his mind played a familiar trick on him. Whenever his mother appeared especially happy, sad, vulnerable, or divine, his father appeared alongside her. For him, they had never ceased to be one.

The girl went inside.

He blew his mother a kiss.

She stretched forth her hand then placed it upon her heart before turning away to go inside.

Though they had lost their appetites for sports of the flesh, Sazar and Numa continued celebrating. Hours flew by as they partied in dance halls, enjoying the rites of passage of red-blooded native sons of the Crescent City. They would repeat these brotherhood rituals countless times, but they would never speak of this night.

Summer came with its waves of heat and restlessness. It came with its legions of vicious mosquitoes and the funky stench from above ground sewers. It came with shirts sticking to armpits and stockings chafing thighs. It came with its chameleon sun shifting from endearing orange to bewitching red. It came as an impetuous reminder that hell is real; and as a warning not to take the milder seasons for granted. It came to scorch and try. Somewhere in its sequence, it came to change things.

Hot and savage. Summertime was not Sazar's favorite season, yet he made the best of it. With secondary school behind him, he looked forward to college in the fall. In the interim he continued his apprenticeship, which would end in July; and he sacked groceries a few mornings a week. The rest of the time he tended the garden, and helped Rose around the house. Reading, collecting, and baseball were his favorite pastimes. He also started escorting Rose to the Jade. They were headed there one evening, when he asked, "Why was she crying?"

"A man that promised to love her—didn't."

"How old is she?"

"I don't know, but she closer to your age than mine." Teasingly, Rose elbowed him, "She's pretty, huh?"

"Really pretty."

"Her name's Jenny. She come from East Texas. Sweet as can be."

"Really?"

"You can say hello to her, if you like."

"I like."

They entered the Jade. Rose started toward the parlor while he stopped to browse the erotic portraits in the foyer.

Rose interrupted his pleasure. "Boy, come on here!" she said, playfully resting her hands on her hips. She took him into the parlor where Jenny and two other women were.

Jenny reclined in a chair with her feet propped on a footstool. When she saw Sazar, she almost sprung from her seat as she poised to sit upright.

With a nod, Rose acknowledged the other women. Then she introduced Sazar to Jenny. "You remember my boy, Sazar?"

"Why yes, Miss Rose. I do. You must be some kind of proud to bring such a pretty thing to the world."

"Pleased to meet you, Miss Jenny. You right lovely yourself."

"Why thank you."

"You're very welcome."

Rose cut her eyes at Sazar, cuing that it was time for him to leave.

"Well, I hope to see you again soon."

In a soft voice peppered with a Southern belle drawl, Jenny responded, "I look real forward to that."

Rose walked Sazar to the door and kissed him on the cheek. "Watch yourself."

He chuckled going down the steps, then glanced back and said, "I will."

Led by insatiable yearnings of the natural and curious kind, Sazar soon found himself visiting Jenny regularly. On Rose's off-nights and behind Viola's back, he slipped into the Jade. He was too naïve to see the affair as dangerous. Up until now his experience with women had not progressed beyond pressing, kissing, and fondling, pleasures that merely wet his appetite. So far his visits with Jenny had gone much the same way. But with her it always felt like a prelude to something grander. He could hardly wait.

Catching his breath, he stood on the Jade's doorstep. It was almost dark, but still very warm out. Quickly, he patted his face with an already damp handkerchief. Then he felt a stinging sensation on his wrist. "Damn!" He swatted a huge mosquito to death and wiped blood on his trousers. Praying that Viola didn't answer the door, he knocked.

A plump woman with a freckled olive complexion and short dark hair greeted him. "How can I help you?"

"Jenny in?"

The woman stepped aside, and pointed to the stairs. "She in her crib."

"She by herself?"

"Would I send you up there if she wasn't?"

"You might," he replied, ascending the stairs.

The door to Jenny's crib was cracked open. She was humming and tapping a comb on the dresser.

Sazar rapped on the door lightly.

"Come in." She twirled around twice then curtsied. "Hey there, handsome."

"How you been?"

"Fine, but better now." She curled up on the bed, and patted the mattress. "Have a seat."

With false reserve, he joined her. At first, she just stared at him. He didn't mind her taking stock of him again. In fact, he liked this part best; seducing women with his looks alone. A power he realized was his when he was still in knee pants. Ever so slightly, he leaned over so she could touch him.

As though he were brand new to her, she meddled at his face. She sighed and wiggled her bare toes up his thigh. Now her wide-eyed gaze turned sultry. He moved in closer. She prowled through his hair in swift broad strokes. Today, her timing was different. He rested on his back. Darting her tongue at his lips, Jenny climbed on top of him and unbuttoned his shirt. Not wanting to tease him too much, she licked his lips and zealously rubbed his chest. When he began to moan, she stretched out and guided his fingers into her mouth to gnaw. They lay meshed in inaugural heat. Slowly, methodically, they tarried in lust.

Face to face. Eyes wide open. No lips, no tongues, just breath. He worked her skirt up and pulled her bloomers down. She stripped off her bodice and corset, freeing her small breast to pleasure his palms. As he progressed to squeezing her torso, she pulled his pants down. They giggled. Somewhere between passion and play, he wound up on top and she helped him inside her.

Soft and generous; all of his fantasies paled. Careful of his own strength, he learned his way around her.

Drenched. They journeyed as far as joy could take them. Assuredly, they arrived together. The bugle call—out of her belly came a chain of babel; he groaned. Afterwards they lay apart in satisfied slumber, but not for long.

Jenny sat up, struck a match on the wall, lit the lamp, and looked at her watch lying on the bedside table. "One of my regulars be here directly." She got out of bed and started dressing; as did a listless Sazar. They went downstairs, and she showed him out. He went to kiss her, but she hurried him off. "See you soon."

"Alright," he said, sauntering into the sweltering darkness.

Sazar's arms were numb from carrying three full sacks of groceries from the quarters to Jenny's house. The course paper next to his chest made the high noon sun feel that much hotter. He didn't mind too much because she seldom asked for favors, so he followed her list to the letter. All those times when he carried her over puddles, held doors for her, escorted her home and complimented her, he was just being himself. She crowned him the most chivalrous man in the world; which had its privileges.

She gave him a key to the shotgun house that she rented in the Ninth Ward, and their liaisons became more frequent. They made all kinds of love. Vigorous love in the morning, hasty love in the midday, fierce love around midnight. They talked too. Little by little, they shared aspirations, histories, and fears. Jenny more so than Sazar, if for no other reason than she was virtually all alone in New Orleans.

He went up the narrow steps, and maneuvered the door open without dropping anything. He made his way to the kitchen and sat the groceries by the pantry. In the icebox he found semi-cool water, poured a glass, and drank it down in one gulp. Still thirsty, he poured another. Desperate to cool off, he fanned himself with open hands, wiped beads of sweat off his nose, and shook out his shirtfront. As he regained his composure, he overheard a frantic voice, Anne's.

She was Jenny's roommate. Extremely shy, Anne was tall, lanky, and dark-skinned with big sad eyes. Morphine had taken a toll on her. Every time Sazar saw her, he felt sorry for her. She looked like a dejected soul that had drifted out of nowhere. She wore Jenny's hand-me-downs. Water was the only thing she put on her face; the same went for her hair. Because her looks relegated her to rank cathouses or worse—rogue pimps, she chose to work from home. "Mister, you give me my due!"

"Ugly as you is, you ought to be free," uttered a slurred voice.

A short fat man stumbled into the dining room with Anne tugging on his arm. Using all his might, he struggled to break free, but she held fast to him. Perplexed by her iron will, he stopped a moment and scratched his baldhead. "Gal, you best let go!"

"Not til I get my pay!"

He took his free hand, balled a fist, and struck her in the mouth. She fell down bleeding and crying.

As quickly as possible, Sazar scanned the kitchen. An iron left cooling on the stove; he grabbed it and rushed to the scuffle. Wielding Herculean force, he rammed the john's face, causing him to wail in agony as layers of his flesh clung to the metal. Between the burns and the booze, he could only muster a haphazard swing at Sazar, and he missed. Sazar kicked him in the groin. The john collapsed on his side. Efforts to get on his feet were thwarted when Sazar propped a foot on his neck, pinning him to the floor. “Let me up,” he groaned.

After watching him squirm for a spell, Sazar reached down and snatched his wallet off him. Then dragging him by the collar and britches, he threw him out into the street.

Right where she had fallen, Anne sat with her face pressed to her knees. Her lip was bleeding and swelling.

Sazar helped her to bed. First he washed her face gentler than she or anyone ever had and applied camphor to the busted lip. Then he poured her a glass of cold punch and fluffed her pillows. She had almost finished her drink and settled into rest, when he gave her the wallet. “Whatever he got, you earned.”

Disinterested, she peeked inside, took out five one-dollar pieces, and gave the wallet back to him. “You earned some too,” she said, snuggling a pillow.

“Rest well, lady.” He left Anne in her room. He found the iron under the dining table. Using his pocketknife and spit, he cleaned it off and sat it back on the stove. Eager to count the spoil, he strutted out the house, locking the door behind him.

When Anne told Jenny of Sazar's valor, the incident affirmed an idea that Jenny had courted from the onset of their relationship: she and Anne could work for him. Calculatingly, she stretched the notion out in her mind; it expanded from favorable to fantastic.

Working for him would provide the physical protection they needed. Book sense and street sense he had. With the fearlessness of youth on his side, he was more likely to take risks that might pan out to be lucrative for all three of them. His good looks would attract a steady stream of girls when the time came. Looking damn near white would give him leverage when dealing with rivals. What could it harm? Time was on his side, so he didn't have to devote all of his youth to vice. The profession might serve as bitter means to a better end. If ever there were an ideal pimp, there was Sazar Jorda. Best of all, Jenny could wash her hands of the rigidity and pettiness that came with working for Viola.

Lo and behold—he must have read her mind. Before Jenny got around to making Sazar a formal proposal, he had taken over Anne. After a few weeks of speculating, Jenny started working for him too.

He oversaw every aspect of the business. He screened the johns. Weapons were seized at the door and returned on the way out. Payments were collected up front. Whiskey was extra, sold by the shot or by the bottle. Tipping the ladies was recommended.

He chose Jenny and Anne's clothing. He had a say on everything from hairdos to bath regimes; he even selected toiletries. The pantry stayed stock full of rice, grits, and oats. At least twice a week, Sazar bought fresh baked pastries and insisted that Anne eat double portions. Soon she picked up weight, her eyes began to sparkle, and her complexion shed a glow. In the wake of her plumper breasts and shapelier limbs, her whole body gave way to a more womanly appearance. Now when Anne looked in the mirror, she didn't slump her shoulders in disgust; instead she admired her shiny braided hair and painted cheeks. Though it was tough going at first, gradually Sazar weaned her off morphine.

Under his management both women made good money; Anne made more that she ever had before. Sazar reminded them that prostitution was not a profession of longevity, and that they should plan for the future, or at the very least a rainy day. So both of them started savings accounts.

The arrangement worked well for him also. The work was easy and the revenues were constant. He and Jenny fooled around less, but their friendship intensified. Where the road might lead never crossed his mind. Perhaps a cavalier attitude was a blessing. Stones that build the temple of one's destiny are easier to carry when not dwelt upon.

Violent rains caught Sazar without an umbrella. Hindered by soaked clothing and mud, he ran down Marais. Finally, he made it home. He kicked his boots off on the porch and hurried inside. He peeled the wet shirt off and hung it on the hallstand. "Ah," he said, catching water in his palm as he slicked his hair back. For a minute he paused and listened to the heavens christen New Orleans. Closely, he listened. There was something about the gait of rain-drenched horses that struck him as phenomenal. Maybe it was how their trots kept time with his heartbeat, or the way their hooves trod the saturated earth. Weren't horses in motion engaged in a dance? Raindrops their serenade?

Chills sprouted over his back and arms, prodding him out of his daydream. Using his foot, he eased the door shut. He was about to remove his pants, when he felt a presence. Nervously, he looked around to find Rose sitting there in the parlor, with her arms folded and a handkerchief in her lap. She didn't say anything. She did not have to. If her taut jaws and cold eyes were any indication, she was mad as hell.

He went to her and tried to take her hand, but she jerked away. "We did not groom you for this."

"Mama, please. I wanted to tell you myself."

"When?"

"Soon."

Her voice unwound like a spool of thread. "Now . . . later, it all hurts the same. Do you know how dangerous this life is? You got to watch yourself and everybody else. The whores, the johns, other pimps. Son, don't be fooled, a whorehouse is the devil's house. One way or another, sorrow comes."

"You do it."

"Cause I had to. I'm doing it strictly for survival. Til you finish your schooling and sit me down."

"I want to sit you down now."

"What about college? The money saved for you to go to Straight. We can keep getting by the way we have."

"I'm not sure I want that right now."

"You used to want it?"

"Not enough to wear out your back."

A volt of rage went through Rose. He had roared (at her), respectively, but roared nonetheless. She stood up, balling the handkerchief in her fist. Hammering each and every word, she said, "You don't know what kind of life this is."

"I'm finding out. But it comes down to this, I won't let you sell yourself to feed a grown man."

"I brought you here. For you, ain't no sacrifice too hard to bear. You all I got."

"Mama, you all I got. You've done this long enough. I can't keep playing schoolboy at the cost of your honor."

"Sazar—"

He put his hands around her shoulders, kissed her forehead, took her by the hand and led her to the settee where they sat together. "Straight will be there when I get there."

"Will you ever get there?"

"Only if I'm meant to." With his mother's feelings in mind, he carefully measured his words. "From now on, I take care of us. Don't ever set foot in Viola's again. Don't worry about me. Understand?"

Tired and wanting sleep but restless from disappointment, Rose closed her eyes and leaned back. Determined to try and deal with her son once more, she cleared her throat and glanced up to see him standing over her. For the first time she saw him through the eyes of a woman. "I may as well."

"Good. I love you lady," he said, bringing her hands to his lips.

Rose retired to Sazar's property across the river in Algiers. With Miss Irene long dead, he was her only tie to New Orleans, so he visited her regularly instead of her coming to him. Her days were spent doing benevolent work. Tending the sick, feeding the hungry, and clothing the naked gave her life additional layers of substance. She attracted lots of gentleman callers, whose company she enjoyed at arm's length.

As for Sazar, over the next decade he reaped prosperity with few interruptions. He purchased a three-story house and renovated it into a bordello. Eventually, his staff grew to fifteen women. He owned three homes in the Tremé, one in the Seventh Ward and land in four parishes. Managing his business, breaking hearts, traveling, and shooting the breeze with Numa filled his days. Yet much of his time was spent engaged in the sport of acquisition. He purchased real estate, art, furnishings, clothing, jewels, horses and carriages. Though his pockets and hours were full, there was a longing that refused to be satisfied by just any old thing. Casually, he drifted from woman to woman, but he still had not loved. So material things became his balm until Agatta.

# 3

## Recess

A time to weep, and a time to laugh; a time to mourn, and a time to dance.
—Ecclesiastes 3:4

Beauty *beauty* is never imposing. Rather it constantly forges new territory to illuminate its grandeur and herald its power.

Playfully, Grace Lorin twirled her purse with one hand, and seductively rested the other on her hip. Her movements were not intended to arouse; her natural stride was a spectacle of glorious tandem. A leg extended in a graceful prowl, a tilt of the head, a bat of the eyes, and a sway of the hips. Knowing that she was hard not to notice, Grace collected the stares of strangers the way Heaven tallied prayers.

Her wiles were striking. One look at her bronze skin brought to mind a yellow rose fired in a kiln. Thick brows perched above piercing black eyes and a pointed nose. A thin lower lip shadowed a pouting upper one. Straight chestnut-colored hair hung down her back. Her anatomy was wonderfully proportioned with a slim waist, heart-shaped hips, and breasts enough.

Sazar spotted Grace across the street, and decided to catch up to her within a block or so.

For almost seven years they had been friends. By chance he and Numa had met Grace and Magdalena one autumn night in a saloon. They were two of the prettiest women that either man had ever come across. Although none of them called it fate, they all agreed that finding each other felt right from inception. Even now they reminisced fondly about their first encounter. The four of them had danced, flirted, and challenged each other's wit. When the music stopped and the smoked thinned, they were bonded. It was late, but the night felt young, so they strolled to Jackson Square and talked until the sun came up.

Sazar fell into a sibling-like relationship with both women. He admired Grace's resilience. She never knew her parents, and had grown up an orphan at the Sisters of the Holy Family Convent. After she left the orphanage, she took up with a veteran who had lost an arm and his mind to the Civil War. Since he made her feel loved, she stayed with him until he died.

Magdalena actually could have passed for Sazar's sister. The spirited blue-eyed beauty had left her grandma and cousins behind in Kisatchie to chase a life that offered more than churning butter, and the prospect of marrying a man that she felt nothing for just to keep a piece of bread in her mouth.

From the start, Numa wooed Magdalena, and she fell hard for the cocoa-colored man with the soft curly hair and sugar on his tongue. It didn't matter that he was the spoiled baby of his family, had made C's in school, and took lady luck for the Holy Grail. He made her feel good.

"Grace!" Sazar called out and waved.

She spotted him. Dodging traffic, he crossed the street to meet her.

They embraced.

He took her hand then stepped back to have a look at her. "Woman there's no end to your charms."

"Why thank you, Mr. Jorda." Hers was a sultry alto voice. She blew words forth like a ripple of slow forming, windblown kisses. "Where you headed?"

"I'm going your way," he grinned coyly, "to see Agatta."

"Really. You know Mam don't want you coming around."

He locked arms with her and they walked together. "Ah . . . dolin', Madam Clovis may wring your nerves to a twit, but not mine."

"What if she catches you?"

"With your help, she won't."

"What about Viv?"

"What about her?"

"You playing a dangerous game."

"We're not as close as we used to be."

Grace stopped, lightly stomped her foot, and said emphatically, "You're not as close to her as you used to be."

"She understands."

"I doubt that."

"Don't," he said, pinching her cheek. Cordially, he took her by the hand and led her up Dauphine.

When they approached No. 51, they waited outside awhile to observe any comings and goings. Finally, Grace made up her mind to go inside. Sazar tried to follow in on her heels, but she stopped him. "Just wait here." She went in and glanced around. Shy of noon on a Sunday, not surprisingly, the parlor was vacant. Mam liable to be gone, she thought. As she was about to return to Sazar, Magdalena and Agatta came downstairs.

"I been looking for you all morning," Magdalena said.

Startled, Grace jumped. "Where's Mam?"

"The room," Agatta answered.

"Sazar outside."

"Whew!" Agatta hurried to the door. Then with her hand on the knob, she gave her heart time to slow down, smoothed her dress out, tossed her hair back, straightened her shoulders, and slowly opened the door. At last, she was visible to Sazar. Coolly, she stood in the doorway.

He rushed over, picked her up, and carried her down the steps. A single kiss transpired into a prolonged act of willful suffocation, which was cut off by a slamming door and hard footsteps.

"No sir, not here!" Zulime shouted.

Grace and Magdalena followed her, and rested on the griffins.

"We 'bout to leave anyway," Sazar responded.

"You know this is trouble." Zulime pointed at Agatta. "More for her than you."

"I'll take care of her," he said, as Agatta hung on his shoulder.

"If Viv don't beat you to it."

"That's my worry, not yours."

"As long as Agatta's under this roof—it's my worry too."

"Fine. Nothing I say or do pleases you."

"Viv is hateful. The girls in your house can't whisper to you, for fear of her."

Growing more frustrated by the second, Sazar paced back and forth, then threw up his hands. "I'm done with Viv."

"Well sir, Agatta, dear I hope you heard that." Proud as a peacock, Zulime strutted down the steps. "You see, when Mr. Jorda is done with a woman, he just moves on. 'Done with her,' he says. I bet she ain't done with you."

"Look, you tend to your business, and let me handle mine. Good day ladies." He kissed Agatta. "Let's go."

Refusing to give up, Zulime adamantly stated, "Jorda, for everybody's sake, I 'preciate if you if you don't come round here no more."

He stopped and turned around. "As long as she lives here, I'm coming by here."

"You really too much." Zulime shook her head. "I can't put up with you."

"Ah, but I can," Agatta said, winking.

"A woman's got to put up with her man!" Grace added.

A defeated Zulime stomped back inside while the others basked in Agatta's liberation and Sazar's victory.

# 4

## Dracon's

But the wicked *are* like the troubled sea, when it cannot rest, whose waters cast up mire and dirt.
—Isaiah 57:20

Dracon's saloon was sanctioned an asylum for colored outlaws. The owner, Able Dracon, sprang from the cradle of Negro mythology. A tall, haunting, graceful man whose dark face was eternally cast in gloom. Always dressed in black, he ran his saloon with the somberness of an undertaker. Around 1875, Dracon showed up in New Orleans, presumably from some other deep Southern state. For three thousand dollars cash, he purchased a dilapidated hall, and spent the next decade cultivating the establishment into a place of beguiling charm.

Black calligraphic letters looped and swirled wickedly on the sign outside, spelling the famed watering hole's name: Dracon's. Round tables were spread throughout the first floor. The bar ran lengthwise the east wall. A cast iron spiral staircase led to the second and third levels. The second floor, known as Bravado Alley because things tended to get rough, consisted of small game rooms. Everything from cockfights to poker games went on up there. Boarding rooms were on the third floor; each room had a cot, small table, lamp, pitcher, and washbowl.

Of course, the main floor was the draw; with its high tin ceiling, black iron chandeliers, Chickering piano, and cement floors. Above the fireplace hung three paintings. One depicted a row of shanty houses surrounded by cotton fields. Another captured linens pinned on a line, blowing in the wind. The central and largest portrait was of an elderly black woman. A red bandana and weathered straw hat composed her crown. Clothed in a white dress, she sat with her gnarled hands clasped around a cane. The deep lines in her face attested to oppression, heartache, and resilience. Soundly, she gazed over yonder.

Folks speculated that Dracon had painted the pictures, and captured his testimony on canvas. He never spoke of his past; and after all, it seemed natural for someone so detached to have an artistic bent. Equally natural was the cry of a man's experience to be emancipated, even if the man himself remained bound.

Yet for all the saloon's intrigue and its clandestine proprietor, Dracon's mystique rested primarily on its metaphysical qualities. Terrible undercurrents of depravity and sadness dwelt in the place. On the surface, seemingly the good times rolled. Cold-blooded desperados drank, good-footed, gambled, and joked. Genuine joy, however, does not exist among corrupt people. They celebrate funerary style. Having made deals with the devil, the wicked are paranoid. For when they least expect it, the Prince of the Air will arrive cloaked in on of his manifold disguises to carry them to the lake of fire. The lawless are ever aware that the word they are yet speaking could be their final adieu, the whiskey on their tongue the last libation, or the present entanglement of flesh the farewell copulation.

On the first floor Agatta, Magdalena, and Sazar sat at a table, finishing their second round. He flagged a young barmaid. She came over and leaned her hip as close to him as she could without making contact.

"Evening folks. What can Madeline get for you?"

"A quart of bourbon." Sazar dropped coins in her hand, moved his chair out of her space, and looked her in the eye. "Keep the change."

"Thank you, Mr. Jorda." Madeline went to the bar and quickly returned with bourbon and three clean glasses.

"You want all of us to love you?" Magdalena asked.

Pouring the drinks, Sazar said, "No such thing as too much love, right?"

"As long as it's the right love," Agatta added.

The three of them raised their glasses in a toast.

"You ladies be real sweet, and I'll dance with you."

Magdalena swallowed some whiskey and tapped her feet. "Girl, we better behave."

As Sazar leaned over to squeeze Agatta's arm, he noticed Numa on the second story balcony with two hoodlums of no small notoriety.

Dag and Cloud. The former went about town in a dingy black cape everyday, regardless of the weather. His brown face was full of deep pits and wild hair sprouted from his wide nostrils. Cloud, Dag's shadow, was slow in the head, stocky, and he had a birthmark that resembled a dark massive cloud splattered over the left side of his face. The mark crested above his eye and trailed off near his mouth. Mostly the pair gambled for their keep and did petty thefts on the side. Like dogs, they camped out under a shed in the swamps. Opium came before food, and anything else for that matter.

The two of them moved about Numa while he stood like a scolded child. Dag pointed in his face, poked his shoulders, and breathed down his neck. During the whole time, Numa kept his eyes to the floor.

"I be right back." Sazar went upstairs. By the time he neared Numa and his adversaries, they were all gazing his way. Systematically, Sazar browsed Dag and Cloud, scrutinizing them from one to the other. Armed with the assuredness that nothing so unsettles vile men as a gentleman's judgment. With an unflinching stare and a stance of superiority, he drove is daggers into Dag and Cloud, and did more damage to their egos than a lifetime of being spurned by pretty women ever could. "What's the problem?"

"Nothin'," Dag said in his husky voice. "Your friend here come across some bad cards."

"Is that so?" Sazar asked Numa.

"Yeah . . . yeah, I reckon it is."

"You let them play you some marked cards?"

"Them cards was fair!" Dag blurted out.

"Like the devil." Sazar reached in his pocket. "How much he owe you?"

"Forty dollars."

"Here." Sazar shoved the bills to Dag.

Gleefully, Dag and Cloud left and shuffled through the loiterers.

"'Preciate it man." Sighing, Numa shook Sazar's hand. "You know I'll pay you back."

"Don't worry about it. Consider it a gift. Watch yourself though."

"I will partner."

"Alright."

As they started downstairs they saw that Numa's foe was not through wreaking havoc.

Dag stood next to Magdalena doing a queer jig, contorting his face, and flapping his cape. Then he grinned like a deranged fool, exposing the broad gaps between his rotten teeth.

Magdalena cringed when the filthy cape brushed her arm.

Inspired by her repulsion, he dared to touch her cheek. Reveling in his stolen pleasure, he did his jig again, and finished his performance with a bow.

Cloud stood aside applauding with his mouth open.

Next Dag attempted to touch Magdalena's hair, but Sazar broke his reach, and spun him around.

"Leave her alone."

"I thought she was free."

"Not to you." Sazar pushed Dag hard, then got in his face. "Go now or leave feet first."

They stood close. Close enough to know exactly where the other was coming from: one from boldness, one from fear.

Dag backed off, and swung his cape high, like a vulture mounting for flight. He turned, swooped down, swiftly rose up again, and mumbled, "She just a high yella ho."

"She worth more than a dead coon."

"Hahhahhahhah . . . " Dag laughed eerily, and fled with Cloud in tow.

"You alright lady?" Sazar asked, tickling Magdalena's ear.

"Good as I'll ever be."

Unsure of how to compensate for his cowardice, Numa pinched her wrist. "She just fine. Girl can raise more hell than you and me both." He rubbed his palms together nervously and took a seat. "She a strong woman."

"Some situations call for a strong man." Sazar sat down and freshened his drink. "When a man gets out of place with your woman, he's gotten out of place with you."

"Ah, partner! That ol' boy just messing round." Numa drank a shot from Magdalena's glass. "Don't start Jorda. You know I'm gon' pay you back."

"I'm not talking about the money. Sure, I don't like you gambling, cause you're no good at it. But when it comes to your lady," Sazar looked at Magdalena, "especially one that's been there for you—you got to stand your ground."

"Come on now. You got your ways, I got mine."

"Yours are wrong." Sazar finished his bourbon and got up. He pulled Agatta's chair away from the table and wrapped his arm around her when she stood.

Numa pinched Magdalena. "You know I love you."

"I do." She kissed him. "You fellas ready to walk us home?"

"Yes ma'am," Sazar answered, blowing into Agatta's ear.

At almost three o' clock in the morning, they left Dracon's. The river was still and the fog was heavy. Sounds of misery and mayhem filled the streets: shattering glass, cussing drunkards, catcalls, and the dwindling dirge of trumpets. At such an hour the city's paradoxical identity reigned. A village of lost and found, forgotten and unforgettable, sacrament and sin, mercy and make do, rendezvous and redemption.

Agatta drew her shawl tightly around her shoulders as she pondered why New Orleans existed at all and why she was (really) planted there. Sazar walked behind her wallowing in her hair.

High on dreams and promises, Numa and Magdalena walked hugged up.

The couples traveled along Conti then turned onto Dauphine. They passed Sazar's brothel; unaware that trouble watched from her tower.

From her bedroom window, lovelorn and intoxicated Vivian Monroe watched Sazar, his friends, and his lover go by. Though she wished she could, it was impossible to deny that Sazar cherished Agatta. Every chance he got he filched a kiss, frolicked in her mane, or caressed her. His hands may as well had been fused to the girl. A man can keep many secrets, but love is not among them. The eyes always tell the tale; the flame kindling in his declared a devotion to Agatta that had blown his mind.

Viv could take no more. Actually, she had seen more than she could handle at first view. Thus, livid was all she could be.

# 5

## Qualm

For of this sort are they which creep into houses, and lead captive silly women laden with sins, led away with divers lusts.
—2 Timothy 3:6

Where had Sazar learned to love? Agatta had posed this question to herself before. She suspected that love came to him the same way it came to her; from way down deep inside, powerfully and precisely.

Alone in her room, she stood idly at the window. Though it was afternoon she still had on her nightclothes. Fatigued by the second day of female time, she had fallen in and out of slumber all morning. Still, she resisted the urge to crawl back into bed. Outside her door she overheard a steady flow a lively conversation, but did not listen for content. Slowly she began to feel awake, so she went to the washstand. As she removed her clothing, the scent of marigolds dizzied her. She cleaned herself, and changed her rags. Then she donned a clean nightgown, wrapped herself in a robe, and retired to the rocking chair.

For almost an hour she rocked in solitude until there was a knock at the door.

"You up?" Magdalena called.

"Yeah, come in."

She stepped inside. Grace and Zulime followed bearing gifts.

"I know you want this." Grace gave Agatta a small brown bag.

"You right." She unwrapped a thick slice of lemon cake.

"Say when." Zulime held a flask of brandy over a hot cup of coffee.

"When."

Zulime sat the coffee on the dresser within Agatta's reach then made herself comfortable on the bed next to Magdalena. Grace relaxed on a trunk.

"So you stayed out late with Mr. Jorda the other night?" Zulime prodded.

"That I did."

"You really not worried?"

"About what?"

"Viv."

"No."

"Child, what in the world is that man telling you?"

"Nothing I don't want to hear. Mam, you the only somebody worried about Viv."

"Well, somebody need to."

"Sazar made it right plain to her that they not in a courting way no more."

"Sure enough?"

"Yeah."

"Ever since Viv showed up at that house. Sazar ain't had room to breathe. I can't believe a woman that hold on that tight, let go this easy."

"Mam, I don't know what Viv's thinking, and I don't care."

"Dear heart, you might care before it's over."

Agatta licked icing off her fingers and sipped some coffee. "It ain't hardly over."

"Girl, you ours. We don't want nothing to happen to you," Grace said.

"I know. I love y'all, and I 'preciate you caring for me."

"Honey," Zulime said, "I don't have nothing against Sazar. Truth be told, I understand you wanting him. Lord knows he something look at."

Magdalena chuckled. "Watch yourself, Mam."

"Oh! The man is alright. Don't ever tell him I said so."

"Umh," Grace added, "we don't need to. Jorda sure enough of hisself already."

Agatta balled up the bag and playfully tossed it to Grace. She sank deep into the chair, smiling blissfully as a child at play. "I'm sure enough of him too."

Viv beat the sun rising. Tripping over her bootlaces, she stumbled up the steps. She had lost her ribbons while dancing; her bright red hair was scattered all over her head. Her bodice was unbuttoned enough to show her flat bosom. Since she had little to lift and was built like a box no matter what, she had decided long ago that corsets were optional. Footprints and debris had soiled the hems of her skirt and petticoat. She reeked of her vices. Overall, she smelled of cigars. She derived great pleasure from propping her elbows on the table, sitting with her legs open, and smoking a fat one. Whiskey tainted her breath. The odor of musky ruffians, with whom she had danced too close to for too long, clung to her and clashed with the cheap perfume that she had earlier rubbed into her skin.

Clumsily, she handled the keys, and was somewhat impressed at how quickly she found the right one. She leaned on the door and entered the house.

In spite of her stupor, instantly she was reminded of why she chose to live and work in Sazar's house. Because he was there. Everywhere. Even in his absence, his masculine bohemian energy pervaded the house. Regardless of how many folks drifted through No. 105 Dauphine, the domain endured as a distinct reflection of his soul.

Essentially, the sitting room was a man's room where women entertained. Torch-shaped sconces lit the arched entrance. A black bearskin rug added a rustic touch. All of the furnishings were ebony; a leather smoking couch, a loveseat, a pair of fireside chairs, and an Empire sofa with brass paw feet. Four paintings hung on the burnt orange walls: two of time ravaged ships and two of sheer black nightgowns.

In Sazar's study, which is where he usually was when at the brothel, books filled the shelves. Carefully placed among the volumes were a few of his model ships, West African statues, and Santeria icons. As far as furniture, he had only what he needed to work and occasionally sleep there. An armoire, a sofa, a pair of savonarola chairs, a black leather-top desk with matching chair, and a curio-cabinet that contained a collection of guns, knives, and rare coins. Sometimes if customers ran short on funds, they bartered with valuables.

Viv peeked through the study's window. Since Sazar was not inside, she turned the doorknob. Unbeknownst to her, Blanche was watching.

"Now, you know better."

"Where is he?"

"Wherever he is, he ain't gone far."

"If folks would mind they own damn business," Viv mumbled. She went to the sitting room, and took a half full bottle of sherry from the bar. Then she slouched down in a chair and drank profusely.

Blanche looked in on her. "You don't give yourself time to sober."

"Leave me alone."

"Cher, you are alone."

The back door opened and closed. Keys jangled. The sound of confident footfalls advanced up the hall.

"Here he come." Blanche whispered.

Gasping, Viv tucked the empty bottle under the chair then thrust herself in the hall.

"Morning, Blanche. Where you headed?" Sazar asked.

"Got a few errands."

"Alright. See you later."

"Bye," she said, utterly singing the word.

He eyed Viv nonchalantly, and walked ahead. Halfway up the stairs, seemingly for no reason at all, he stopped. He stroked his hair back, folded his arms, and stood contemplatively. Under the precept that Viv hated silence, he used it to unnerve her.

Not knowing what to say or do, she waited and loathed herself for adoring a man who was as hard to hold as a snowflake (for her anyway). Now, like so many times before, she wished she could store away her feelings for him or at least make them hush. But her love for him was mightier than she and equipped with its own volcanic will. Being drunk and half crazy failed to null her sentiments. If she had been blind, maybe she could have left him alone.

Pomade glistened in his hair. His face was clean-shaven. Dressed in a dark red shirt, tobacco brown-trousers, and calfskin boots; he was the picture of an urbane adventurer.

Hopelessly smitten, Viv studied him.

Finally, he faced her. Half irritated, half amused. He asked, “You on the rag?”

“Naw.”

“Why don’t you let alone the spirits, get washed up, take a nap, and be ready to work later on.” He started up the stairs again.

“I saw you the other night.”

“So.”

“With Agatta Lugar.”

He came to a halt, and leaned over the banister. “That’s none of your business. Stay in your place, if you want to keep working here.”

"Umh, umh, umh," she groaned. Slow, heavy tears fell from her eyes. A ball of hurt lodged itself in her chest. Paining to stabilize her speech, she stammered. "I . . . I . . ." Then her voice found a strain of conviction. "I saw you loving her with your eyes. Now you stand here looking at me like I'm dirt. Oh! It's easy to tell when a man done moved on. He go to looking at you different." She sauntered to the bottom of the stairs, and shouted. "Now your eyes don't like me no more. Cause they loving her just like the rest of you."

"Get cleaned up."

"You see some lil' girl left in her face, so you want to protect her. You ready to rescue somebody, but not a woman that's whoring for you."

"You were a whore when I met you. Working for me was your notion. I never asked you to—I never would have."

"I may not be the best woman in the world, but I care for you." Viv looked to the ceiling, squinting at its height. Quick as lightning she planted her gaze back on Sazar. She wiped her cheeks then danced a hula dance. Gradually her movements evolved into a ring-around-a-rosy minus the squat. Next she raised her skirt slightly and pranced on her toes. Her eyes were closed so tightly that lines formed at their corners. With a hand on her forehead, she scrounged her memory to recollect something of grave importance, and kept searching until she had a firm hold on the subject matter. "I dream the day when a man look at me the way you look at her. You know, my daddy, rest his soul, used to look at my mama like that. Yeah! I had a mama and a daddy too." She sashayed, fanning her hands wildly.

"He would romance Mama a thousand times with his looking eyes before he said a word to her or gave her his touch. She was his everything. I used to think she had a hex on him. In her heyday, Simone Monroe was a beautiful woman. Lord! She knew it."

Stooped over, Viv breathed hard like she was going to vomit. Little by little she straightened her back. "Mama come from Martinique. A tall woman. Black as coal, soft as velvet. When she look at you with those dark eyes, feel like she looking straight through you. White her favorite color. Everything in her boudoir the color of snow. She would sit in the middle of her bed, and take her raiments off slow as molasses. Angel on a cloud; would stir Daddy for sure. Yeah them island women something else.

"You know how they move. Never in a hurry. Love they bodies. Ain't scared of nothing. First time I saw Mama dance naked in the moonlight, I was a lil' bitty girl. Every part of her teasing that ol' moon. Ah, but she knew how to look right at the sun. Always up fore daybreak to start her doings. The ol' sun must've told her she was queen of them all. She was something else—still is. Even her walk was a dance. That woman moved like she was loving herself a lil' more every step of the way.

"You know what I'm talking 'bout. Proud, beautiful woman. Like your mama, Miss Rose.

Them woman can be right close to you and still be far away. They stir your soul. Is that how you see Agatta? She stir your soul?"

"Go wash up."

In vain, she sobbed again. His indifference further upset her already fragile temperament. She sank to the floor, and caught tears in her lap. "Can't you see how much I love you?" She pulled her skirt and petticoat up by her thighs and crawled aimlessly. The maple pinched her knees. Yet for two good reasons she preferred that discomfort over heartache. First, the pain affirmed that she was still flesh and blood. Secondly, all she had to do was stand to ease that pain. "Agatta done touched your soul. When a woman do that . . ." Viv fell forward on her elbows as her heart and voice broke to pieces.

# 6

## Men

Honour all *men.* Love the brotherhood. Fear God. Honour the king.

—1 Peter 2:17

Shopping for produce at the French Market was always a cathartic excursion for Agatta. She marveled at the brilliant colors and superb forms. She found it amazing that fruits and vegetables were both edible and lovely to behold. Awed that each and every one of the provisions were yielded of the earth. Some sprang from dust, some sprouted on vines, others swelled on trees. All had a skin, flesh, serum, and a core; when ripe, they were sold at marketplace.

Eagerly she moved down the isle to a crate of coconuts. She wasn't serious about purchasing one; the milk was too sweet unless she craved it. She placed her hand among the pile of browns and compared their pigments to her own. Soon she found a close match, and picked it up for further examination. Its dark brown husk gave her the comfort she longed for—commonality. The coconut fit perfectly in her hand. She held it up to her ear, shook, and listened to the tide of its milk. Purely for play, she shook it again, then carefully returned it to the crate. But her hand, as though awaiting the proper moment to separate, clung to the fruit. Actually, her mind wandered off.

She could slip into fantasia anywhere, at anytime, and the catalyst could be anything. Random occurrences, from the trivial to the sublime could send her thoughts reeling. During such times, the only way to lure her out of the daze was to invade her space.

Someone was trying to.

The smell of shaving soap tickled her nostrils; warranting her attention away from the fruit. Then, in a voice that gave her chills, the stranger said, "It ain't near 'bout as pretty."

Agatta was too stunned to face him right away. His pitch ranged between a howl and a moan. It was strong yet equally consoling. She scanned her history but she found nothing to compare that voice to. What he looked like failed to matter; vocally he had been blessed enough. She looked up. "You don't think so?"

"No ma'am, I know for sure." Tipping his hat, he extended his hand, and said, "Luther McBride."

His voice fit. He was black. Blue-black and smooth. Bald. Slightly taller than her man and robust. When he smiled, his eyes disappeared; he reminded her of the laughing Chinamen on the posters. He was not a young man, but he wasn't old either. His eyebrows were still dark. Whether or not he was good-looking, she couldn't say. But drawing power—now that he had.

"Pleased to meet you. Name's Agatta Lugar." She flagged an elderly vendeuse, and put her goods on the counter as the woman came over to assist her. She paid for a half a dozen bananas, a bunch of grapes, and a bunch of cherries. "Merci."

Luther asked, "You mind if I walk with you?"

"No sir, I'd be obliged."

They moved easily along the market's lightly populated isles, and walked out to Decatur Street.

It was a clear day, gifted with soft breezes, and a wide-eyed sun. The kind of day that dangled a promise or two.

At first she felt awkward walking with a man other than Sazar, but her uneasiness quickly passed. Still, she half hoped that Luther would abandon her before they reached Dracon's, where Sazar would be waiting. Hope's other half wanted to know more about the man with the trombone voice. "You live in town?"

"I do. Not far from here."

"You work close by?"

"Sure do. At Immanuel Tabernacle, on Robertson before you get to La Harpe."

"You a preacher?"

"Yes, the pastor."

"I'm no saint."

Luther laughed. "Don't go blotting your name from the roll just yet."

"I reckon it's been blotted for me."

"No sister, as long as you here, there's grace enough to cover you."

"It takes a whole lot of grace to sanctify a harlot."

"My God's got it."

"Is it your custom to befriend scarlet sisters?"

"I befriend just about anybody."

"Even lost souls?"

"Miss Agatta, you not lost—you just lost your way."

"You aim to help me find it?"

"You'll get home whether I lend a hand or not, though I'd be right honored to help. I imagine you much closer than you think."

"To tell the truth, I never thought on it."

"Sometimes that's the best way to get close. Just know that God covers you and loves you."

"Sure sounds good."

"It is."

They crossed onto Conti and neared Dracon's. Agatta saw Sazar out front, leaning on a post. They locked eyes, but she could not pinpoint his mood.

He was not a jealous man, nor was he intimidated by other men of any sort; he was, however, territorial. Women, possessions, space—anything that he laid claim to was best left to him and him alone.

Sazar pivoted around the post, and kind of swayed back on his right heel. Careful not to let it show on his face, he pondered the man walking with Agatta. A man who clearly was not sweet on her.

She perked up like a little girl approaching her favorite doll. Luther honed in on her sudden excitement and the energy between her and Sazar. “Is that your beau?”

“Yeah.”

“Y’all make a fine looking pair.”

“Why, thank you.”

They crossed Chartres, and in no time they were face to face with Sazar.

“Good afternoon,” she said.

“It’s better now.” He bent sideways to kiss her cheek.

She turned to her new acquaintance. “Reverend Luther McBride, meet Sazar Jorda.”

“Pleased to meet you,” Luther said.

They shook hands.

“Likewise.” Bewildered, Sazar took a step back and glanced from Luther to Agatta and back again. He raised an eyebrow, “Reverend,” he said, folding his arms and surveying the surroundings, “this is a strange place to spread the good news.”

“I beg to differ. It’s the perfect place. Church folks already saved. It makes good sense to minister to those who’ve gone astray.”

“Maybe they strayed to where the need to be.”

“If so, they’ll stay there.”

“I see. But surely there’s enough work to do around your church house.”

“Oh! Indeed there is, but you see—everything under the sun is God’s, so his work is everywhere.” Luther smiled as he looked Sazar right in the eye.

"Ministry can be trying work sometimes, yet it reaps the sweetest rewards."

"I imagine so; especially when you have nothing else to do."

"Man has but two labors, the Lord's work or the devil's."

Sazar took Agatta by the hand and coaxed her close to him. "That must be some narrow-minded man." Cavalierly, he nodded farewell.

"Good day, Mr. Jorda. Miss Agatta."

"Bye," she said softly.

Beneath a cloudless sky the cool halcyon waters of Lake Pontchartrain rippled as gently as a stray breeze along the spine or the sigh of a baby during siesta. Secluded by columns of oak trees draped in Spanish moss, the lake was a longtime gathering place for lovers, religious rituals, picnics, reunions, and retreats. Whether solo or accompanied, the lake held the ace of all aces—it never talked.

Sazar drove to an isolated realm of the lake and parked in the marsh. He roped the horses to a tree, leaving enough slack for them to graze and drink. He waited for Agatta to take off her shoes then helped her out of the carriage.

They undressed. As usual, she was naked first because eyeballing her delayed him. She winked at him, covered her breasts, and walked toward the shoreline. Her hands fell to her sides. Squinting at the sun, she plunged into the water, an ethereal enigmatic mermaid at play in paradise.

He dove in and swam after her. They splashed about for the longest time, then held hands and floated in circles. She threw her head back and closed her eyes. Around and around they spun until she grew dizzy. Next they raced. After six laps of vigorous competition, they drifted back to each other. She laced her legs around his waist and let her arms drape his shoulders while he clutched her rear. Lost in one other's eyes, they held that stance.

Sazar pecked Agatta on the lip and touched off a series of rapid kisses. Now they were stirred and anxious to get *there.* Two ecstatic lovers in too big a hurry, so all they could do was play and play they did.

They fell away laughing. She floated on her back while he drew signs on her belly and explored her navel with his tongue.

For hours, they charmed and frolicked until lethargy crept upon them. Now the waters burdened their limbs as they swam back to shore, and fell asleep on a blanket.

They woke up famished, and feasted on fruit, fried pork skins, and lemonade.

With their stomachs satisfied, they lay curled together. "I love you," he said.

"Why?"

"I don't know. I just do."

"You're a man of mystery."

"I'm a man of truth. The first time I saw you it was like seeing the rest of me come home. The best of me at that."

"Good enough." She snuggled in his arms.

They lay awhile longer and watched as the sun turned dark orange and sank below the horizon. A locust perched stubbornly on their blanket. Nearby a pigeon devoured a worm for supper.

"I could lay here forever, but we better go," he said.

"What constitutes forever?"

"Til one of us leaves the earth."

"That could be a mighty long time."

"Be it another day or a hundred years from now, I want to spend it with you."

"Fine by me."

They sat up and Sazar gathered Agatta's hands to kiss her palms. As poised as Aphrodite, she lounged under the shifting sky. Once more she bewitched him. This time the birthmark was to blame. He found it delightfully baffling how nature could be so random, yet so precise. Centered, distinctly darker than her coloring, and perfectly round. Seemingly such a small thing, but it was integral to her lure. Though she would have been beautiful without it, with it she was magnificent.

"I love you. All of you." He kissed the enchanting mark.

"All of me?"

"Yes, the good, the bad, and things I cannot name."

"Are there things you can't name?"

"Umh, umh." He smirked and pinched her thigh.

"Your affection is all joy to me. I'm glad you find comfort in mine."

"Dolin', rest assured, I do."

They kissed.

"Come on girl. It's getting late. We better hurry."

Reluctantly, they dressed and collected their belongings.

# 7

## The Black Nightgown

For a whore *is* a deep ditch; and a strange woman *is a* narrow pit.

—Proverb 23:27

Awakened by the visitation of aggressive winds shifting the swag and a stream of daylight glaring in her face, Viv sluggishly rolled over on her stomach. She kicked away the covers, rubbed mucus out of her eyes, and began studying the carvings on the headboard. She was not, however, admiring the original craftsmanship, but her own handiwork.

One of the masterfully chiseled pineapple finials was riddled with her intentional flaws. Every time she and Sazar made heat in her bed, she opened her pocketknife and drove a tiny blade into the wood. Regardless of how hungover she was, if she managed to see morning in that bed, ritually she tried to tally up the notches. But she never counted past thirty-seven because something always interrupted her, like the need to piss or a growling stomach; yet far more frequently the arithmetic triggered a flashback that demanded her full consideration. Whereas on this morning, she simply felt bad. So she let alone the numbers and took on the formidable task of getting out of bed.

With her skull throbbing like steel was being towed through it, Viv sat up and stretched her sore limbs. Her tongue was laden with a chalky stale-tasting film. Sporadic coughing did little to relieve her dry throat. She felt pain between her legs, but could not recall why. She scooted along the edge of the mattress, stationing herself in front of the cheval glass, where she commenced another ritual: idolizing the black nightgown.

The gown was very becoming. Satin and long with a V-neck that plunged to her navel and a hem that dusted her feet in an elaborate fishtail.

Sazar had purchased it for her from a traveling salesman. She coveted the gown more than anything else she owned. More than her matching cameo brooch and earrings. More than her mother's pearl necklace. She loved the gown so much that she knew its whereabouts at all times. Instead of handing it over to the washerwoman along with the rest of her laundry, Viv washed the gown herself, pinned it to the clothesline on her balcony, and never left home until it was dried, folded and tucked safely away in her bureau.

Often she judged her weight according to how the gown fit. She would wiggle and sashay before the mirror. If the gown looked or felt too snug, she would abstain from bread pudding. Every question or answer she had regarding her desirability rested on that which the nightgown revealed. In it she found a veritable satin crystal ball.

She stepped up to the mirror. Back and forth she swayed. In spite of her misery, she hummed sketchily. During this bliss she smiled. For a fleeting moment she actually felt better, then she got a good look at herself. Suddenly the scope of her ruin confronted her.

She quit waltzing and looked closer at a reflection that horrified and saddened her. Like wheels of tribulation, dark heavy circles squatted under her eyes. The sheen was fading fast from her curly red hair. Once rosy and plump, now her freckled cheeks were dull and sunken. She could not remember the last time that she really looked good. Curiously she slid the gown off her shoulder; the reddish saffron-hued skin there was as sullen as the rest. She sank to the floor and wept. Hoping that she had overlooked some trace of vitality, she clutched the mirror and pressed her face to the unforgiving glass. To her disappointment, the view up close was worse. Even through a shroud of tears she could see webs gathered at the corners of her eyes and deep lines at the sides of her mouth where the cutest dimples used to be. Every hard road that she ever traveled had paved its testimony into her brow.

The cold-blooded truth: the gown was in fine condition; the woman, however, had gone to the dogs. I look like and old *old* ass woman, she thought. She eased away from her reflection, and crawled haphazardly trying to make sense of all the lost yesterdays somersaulting in her mind. So she teetered between regret and anger, but she needed to settle on a single emotion; the former would take her to deeper depths, the latter would take her elsewhere. She got to her feet and stepped out into the hall, where the only thing stirring was a ray of sunshine. Undetected, she rushed downstairs to Sazar's study.

Frantically she wrestled with the knob, then shoved herself against a door that was as unyielding as his heart. "You in there?" she ranted. She put an ear to the door. Not a sound. Despite feeling fatigued, she mustered the energy to continue searching downstairs. Had she relied on the stamina of her weary constitution, she might have folded. But love and rage are strong persuaders. She pressed her way to the kitchen.

A lukewarm pot of coffee sat on the stove. She left it there and went to the sitting room, where Abby sat alone smoking a cigar.

Like Viv, Abby had grown up in Thibodeaux. Their families were acquainted. Not long after Viv arrived in New Orleans, she ran into Abby on the street. Both of them found comfort in seeing someone from back home. They exchanged addresses. Soon Viv had someone to confide in. Although their temperaments were like night and day, Abby was the closest thing to a best friend that Viv ever had.

She was sound minded, not given to whining and bickering. Her conversation was usually brief and to the point. If she had any aspirations or disappointments, she kept them to herself. As for men, she neither praised nor scorned them. She didn't have a steady beau, and never mentioned wanting one. She had more female clients than any of the other girls; almost half of her clients were women.

A handsome woman. Her skin was the color of honey. She wore her coarse hair in cornrows, a kerchief typically covered it. Her wardrobe was architectural and basic. She seldom strayed from dark colors.

"Where he at?" Viv asked.

"He ain't here," Abby answered, blowing a double ring of smoke.

"You seen him?"

"Not since yesterday, early."

"Umh," Viv sighed. She stretched from side to side before arching her back and creating a conduit for pain to travel up to her neck. I must have fell down, she contemplated. Nervously, she tugged at her hair and walked to the window. She peeked behind the curtain. The street was unusually full. But what struck her as odd were the throngs of women dressed in pastels and flaunting hats that resembled bouquets and laughing children scurrying about with brightly colored stuffed baskets. "Why all the rainbow fanfare?"

"It's Easter," Abby said.

"Oh."

"You need a bath. If Jorda catch you looking like this, he'll have a fit."

"I need a word with him."

"Girl, you can't wait at that window for him all day. Man's where he wants to be." Abby put out her cigar and went to Viv's side. "It's time to move on."

"All the time I spent loving him."

"It's still time."

"No."

"He has."

"So."

Like a soft prong, Abby's fingers coddled Viv's chin, guiding her face away from the window. "So—you have no choice, cher."

"I don't know what else to do."

"All you have to do is *leave* him alone."

"It ain't that easy. Every time I see him . . ."

"Maybe you need to move way from here since you can't handle seeing the man everyday. You certainly can't keep carrying on like this."

Viv hung her head low then looked away. Despairingly, she mumbled, "You just don't know." Her gaze bounced from one street scene to another as she resumed twisting her hair.

"I hate to see you like this, but if you won't—"

"Leave me alone."

Seeing no point in pressing the matter, Abby obliged and let her be.

Nagged by a growling stomach, Viv stroked her belly and imagined lunch possibilities. Hard as she tried, she failed to recall yesterday's provisions or if she supped at all. After all, her custom was to drink more and eat less. She decided to ponder meals during her bath. She took half a step back as the curtain slowly cascaded over the window, then out of nowhere something captured her attention. She pressed her nose to the glass. Sure enough it was Sazar. He was with Agatta. They were holding hands.

As sick as seeing them together made her, she felt compelled to watch. A helpless bystander, she spectated as her devalued affections were fed to her raging bonfire heart. But what could she do? Look away (part of her wanted to)? Let go? *Hell naw!* She waited and watched; when her nerves permitted mobility she hurried upstairs to her crib.

She jerked open drawers and rummaged through garments. Finding nothing to work with there, she moved on to search the wardrobe. Again nothing. Desperate, she got down on her knees and investigated under the bed. She found a long forgotten hatbox. Inside she discovered a wide brim hat, a pearl hatpin was tucked below the plume; she seized it, and crawled over to the slop jar to spit. A second wind came over her. Quickly, she got to her feet and hastened downstairs.

In the kitchen she sifted through cigar boxes that contained silverware. Lots of paring and butter knives turned up, but those were useless. Next she explored the cupboard, but the meat cleaver eluded her, as did the carving and butcher knives.

Agitated and pressed for time, she clutched the hairpin and ventured to Sazar's study. Despite a shaky hand, she pried open the lock. She scurried about aimlessly before settling on the curio cabinet that held Sazar's knife collection. Again she employed the hatpin, but this lock wouldn't budge. So she slid behind the cabinet and hurled it to the floor. She held her breath as the glass shattered and the contents dispersed. From the ruins she retrieved a thirteen-inch dagger with a leather-clad handle and a blade with a curved tip.

Ever mindful of timing and her bare feet, she crept out of the study, through the foyer, out of the house.

The sun stung her tear-clouded eyes; though she refused to weep. Her demons morphed into a stone pillar, the weight of which pressed down on her skull. Now every intense step exacerbated the pain. She feared the headache would be the death of her before she even reached Agatta. Blinking rapidly to clear her vision, she browsed the crowds methodically seeking Agatta, who happened to stand out because in a profusion of pale shades, she wore a royal blue dress and African violets adorned her braided upswept hair.

She and Sazar were parting and even their good-bye embodied foreplay. The way they released each other's fingers was no different than a banana relinquishing its peel. At last, Agatta turned away and walked ahead. Sazar went to the opposite direction toward Viv.

Cleverly veering away from the thick of traffic, Viv moved along the inner fringe of the sidewalk and trailed Agatta.

Sazar walked several blocks before he noticed clusters of people casually stepping aside in unison, apparently clearing a path; he didn't think much of it. He passed right by Viv, but the crowds blotted her from his sight. Curious as to why folks were swerving, he glanced back a few times. Then he heard someone say, "That gal got a knife." Though a little trepidation swelled in his gut, rationale quelled it. However, he did an about face and surveyed the hoards anyway. Every so often people still filed either to the left or right, yet the catalyst eluded him. Nevertheless, he focused. Then, in turns and phases like the wildly shifting scenes of a nightmare, a manifestation. First he recognized the crown of unruly flaming hair. Next the familiar gait revealed itself; the pure friction of grinding hip motion and hard flat-footed steps. Lastly, his gaze descended upon the lingerie that he knew all too well. In a sea of watercolors—the black nightgown. A bat out of hell flung down on flamingo paradise. There she was, a nimble satin-cloaked Mephistopheles—Viv.

Sazar pursued her.

Though he couldn't see Agatta, she was all he thought of. He walked as fast as possible, but there was no such thing as a clear straight path. To make matters worse, Viv had quite a lead on him and marched like a brave. At every angle something thwarted his efforts to make headway. There were decrepit old folks and frolicking children to contend with. People strolled elbow to elbow as though they didn't have a care in the world. After all, it was Resurrection Sunday all day long. While Sazar was alienated at calvary, everyone else proceeded in sanctimonious parade, basking in the glow of an Everlasting Father.

Though it was difficult to do with Agatta weighing heavily on his heart, and big fancy hats blocking his view, he kept track of Viv. But she messed with his mind. His gravest sorrows resonated and vied for grieving space. *The marine hearse transporting his father's ghost . . . his mama on the block . . . now his beloved, vulnerable prey for a lunatic with a blade.*

He decided to go through an alley that led to Burgundy Street, hoping there would be less traffic, so that he might cover greater distance and file back onto Dauphine up ahead. He planned to either stop Viv or rescue Agatta or at the very least get between them.

Dodging vagabonds, trash barrels, and stray goats, he cut swiftly though the lane. Luckily there was less fanfare on Burgundy. He sprinted past rows of charming townhouses, then dashed through a breezeway that brought him to the corner of Orleans and Dauphine. Frantically, he looked every which way until he saw Viv.

By now she had less of a lead and he was certain that he would catch her. Quickly, he slipped past small groups wherever he found an opening. Finally, he got close enough to leap and seize Viv by the hair—maybe.

Too old for such lavish Easter baskets, three girls strolled shoulder to shoulder. Their tight shiny sausage curls bouncing as they grinned and giggled, oblivious to the danger in their midst and everything else.

Sazar stepped off the curb. Out of nowhere a begging child towing a cripple in a makeshift wagon wandered in his path.

Viv was quick. In moments she had advanced her footing. Bombarding about the huddles, exiting the sidewalk when called for, strategically zooming by carriages. Treading the ground on bare feet, she prowled effortlessly past slowpokes. About six people separated her from Agatta. She was close enough to see the pretty lace detail on Agatta's sleeve. She positioned herself to get within striking distance.

With his heart threatening to burst from his chest, Sazar ran down the middle of the street. He managed to get near Viv again; only a few clusters of people divided them. But she was that much closer to Agatta. For the first time he had full view of both women. Room to capture Viv was limited. Bumping into the strangers in front of him, he chanced reaching out to grab her hair. Just as his middle finger grazed a fiery curl, he felt some playful commotion at his knees. Rambunctious twin boys scampered by, stepping on his toes, and smearing his pants with lollipops. By the time they were out of the way, Viv was inches away from Agatta, and well beyond Sazar's reach. Lord let her heed my voice, he prayed. "Agatta run!"

Completely unaware of the danger, Agatta turned around. Though Sazar's anguished expression bewildered her, she smiled. Her lips parted to speak when Viv stuck the knife in her side, and in an instant withdrew the bloodstained weapon with flesh dangling from its tip.

Agatta staggered and shielded her wound with both hands. Trembling, she examined the red on her fingers. A bad stinging sensation escalated to excruciating pain that wracked her whole torso. Back and forth she teetered before collapsing.

Sazar accomplished getting his hand on Viv as she prepared to attack again. They wrestled until he stood behind her, choking her and pinching her wrist. Kicking and bucking, she endured the pressure on her veins as long as she could; but inevitably couldn't, so she surrendered and let the weapon fall to the ground to be buried under his foot. He shoved her away and tucked the knife in his waistband.

She hobbled about gasping, holding her neck. She caught enough breath to compose a curse. "Damn you both! You'll never know a moment's peace!" Void of any remorse, she stomped her way past the small crowd that had gathered.

Two passersby were aiding Agatta. She rested her head in the lap of one, who consoled her, "You gon' be just fine." Another applied pressure to the wound with a shawl.

Now Sazar hovered over Agatta, caressing her face. "How bad?"

Her eyes were clinched shut; she writhed in the dirt. "Bad."

The lady with the shawl uncovered the wound and slightly backed away, allowing Sazar room to view. He touched the cut, trying to gauge the depth of the wound. Blood, thick and warm, saturated his fingers. "It's not that bad, dolin'." He leaned into her ear, speaking softly and slowly, "I'll lift you as gently as I can. But it's gon' hurt worse.

"I know."

The Samaritan wrapped the shawl around Agatta's waist and tied her purse strings to her wrist.

"Thank you both kindly," Sazar said.

"You ready?"

"Yeah."

"Bear with me baby." He raised Agatta and flinched when she drove her nails into his back and loosed a scream that pierced his ears and tortured his heart. "Ahhhhh!"

Her shrill cry waned to moans, but the harrowing song of her battered soul would haunt him for the longest time. "Love, I'm so sorry. Please forgive me," he pled.

"Don't let me die."

"I won't . . . for nothing in this world."

"I'm still bleeding."

"Not as much. Dr. Thezan just right up the way. We'll make it. He kissed her on the temple. "You be like new in no time."

Her breathing slowed. Trustingly, she looked into his eyes. Her severed flesh bled and throbbed; she lost consciousness when the pain was too much to bear.

# *8*

# Agatta's Testimony

Man *that is* born of a woman *is* of few days, and full of trouble.

—Job 14:1

Air seeped through the bandages and into Agatta's stitched wound. She wiggled a little to soothe the itching. After a week she had learned to balance her weight to avoid the worst of the pain; but the torn flesh was still quite sore. Supporting herself on her elbows she sat up and rested against the headboard.

Sal had already taken the bedpan, so Agatta waited for Mam, Grace, and Magdalena. Every morning they came to comb her hair, dress her wound, feed and bathe her, and make not so subtle attempts to demystify her past. That was all right; their prying no longer made her nervous. She was grateful for all they did.

She counted her blessings: twice she had cheated death, good women cared for her, and the man she loved loved her.

She missed Sazar. By Grace, he had sent two lovingly apologetic letters. In his splendid longhand he gave her much to look forward to; thereby hastening her recovery. His words stayed with her like the memory of a butterfly resting on her face, or her mother calling her by her full name (meaning that she had better come *right now*), or the caress of warm sand on her calves, or the first time that she put her hands on her hips and let her backbone . . . until her cheeks teased the ground.

His words stayed with her:

*My darling Agatta,*

*I hope that you will someday forgive me. Your suffering is due only to my negligence. I cherish you, and would gladly lay down my life that you might live. I pray for your quick recovery, and assure you that Vivian will not trouble either of us again. Grace and Magdalena will keep my informed of Zulime's temperament, mercurial soul that she is. As soon as I get word of her mellowing, I will call upon you.*

*Yours always,*
*Sazar*

She speculated that he would call on her before Zulime settled; she hoped so. She harbored nothing outside of love for the man and could hardly wait to show him so.

Strangely, she held no bitterness toward Viv; although she was woefully inconvenienced and perplexed. She wrestled with the unexplained phenomenon of a jilted woman seeking revenge on her former beau's new flame while leaving him intact as though he were protected by some lover-man immunity.

She tossed the covers aside, stretched her numb legs, and twinkled her toes. Cautiously she stretched her arms then unbraided the single plait in her hair. She had not yet mustered up the courage to look at the wound in her side. Having never been scarred, her reluctance stemmed from fear and vanity. Before she had been a religious practitioner of self-adoration; now she would postpone disrobing before a mirror—at least until the scab fell away. Already she missed basking in her nude reflection. Getting naked for Sazar was another bridge to cross altogether. The issue was not whether he would receive her body. But now she bore a permanent reminder of what went wrong in their history; one that cut seven centimeters deep and three inches ugly. It would take time for both of them to get used to.

Dr. Thezan offered his best consolation when he stitched her up. He said that scars tended to fade and shrink over time; then in the same breath he stated matter-of-factly that she could count on carrying this one to her grave. Of course, Mam's prognosis sounded far more promising. She assured Agatta that the mark would lighten because she was young and they were going to treat it with bee earring oil and dew-drenched plantain leaves. That was Mam, queen of golden prospects.

The shutters were open and morning swarmed the room, beckoning Agatta to wellness. She asked herself, how could anybody ever get enough morning? With each and every glint of sunglow her thoughts delved deeper into life's raw purpose and pleasure: living for life's sake and finding *whatever* joy therein.

She heard the benevolent brigade marching down the hall, so she put on her gayest face. Though some days she felt like she had one foot in the crypt, her friends needed to know that they were indeed nursing her back to good health.

Rapping softly on the door, "You up dolin'?" Zulime asked.

"Yeah, come in."

"You must be feeling better." Zulime rolled up her sleeves.

"I am."

"You be better than that after a swig of this good old chickory," Grace said.

Magdalena sat a tray across Agatta's lap, gave her a napkin, and served her breakfast. Scrambled eggs, fried bacon, and hot grits covered the plate. The more she smelled the food, the hungrier she grew. She drank some coffee and dug in.

Casually Grace ran a feather duster over the dressing table while Magdalena swept the floor.

Zulime sat in a chair next to the bed. "You coming along fine."

"Cause I have y'all to look after me."

"You beat death . . . twice?"

"Twice," Agatta held up two fingers, smiling from one side of her mouth.

"The Lord not through with you."

Magdalena propped the broom in a corner, tiptoed over to Agatta, and gently tickled her underarm. "If a cat got nine lives, you must have ten."

They all laughed.

"She got this one for sure," Zulime added.

Swallowing the last of her coffee, Agatta agreed. "That I do."

Grace finished dusting. She put a hand behind her hip, and poked out her chest to stretch her back. Then she poured water in the washbowl, unwrapped a bar of castile soap, and collected the medicines prescribed by Dr. Thezan.

"Here," Zulime said, taking a small pouch from her apron, "put this in the bath."

"What's this?" Grace asked.

"Herbs to help close her up."

Grace passed the pouch under her nose. "Chamomile's strong." She sprinkled the herbs and stirred a sponge in the bath.

"It's in there. Just be glad you don't need it."

"I'm full." Agatta sighed, pushing her plate aside.

"You strong enough to move? Or you want to stay put?" asked Zulime.

"I'd like to move around some."

"Good. We can change the sheets."

Grace and Magdalena supported Agatta's upper body, Zulime held her legs, and they carried her to the chaise.

Changing locations gave the infirmed some exhilaration. She perked up even more as Magdalena massaged oil into her scalp and brushed her hair.

With great expediency, Zulime stripped the bed while Grace gathered clean linens from the chest. Together they tucked and smoothed with a zeal that reminded Agatta of her mother, Addy Lugar. Like Zulime, Addy regarded housework as a sacred art.

Zulime's hands captured Agatta's gaze; like Addy's, they were dexterous and beautiful. Zulime's fingers were short and plump with prominent knuckles and baby soft. Deep lines mapped her palms. Bold sapphire rings often adorned her fingers. Her hands made her interesting and lively. A simple wave on her part evolved as grandly as a dove taking to the sky. Every now and then she danced around No. 51, napping her fingers, and clapping with such enthusiasm, savvy, and rhythm that her hands transformed into invaluable percussion instruments. A fierce debater, she expressed many a fine point with those hands. Surely they were designed to grapple with the issues of life: people, communication, and industry.

Grace was shaking the folds out of the top sheet when Zulime preempted her, snatching the sheet, and wildly shaking it in the air. Thrice she sent it soaring before allowing it to settle on the bed.

All of them fell out in riotous laughter. "Cool her down, Mam," Magdalena chuckled.

Stooping over, Grace held her belly, barely able to speak for laughing. "What in the world come over you?"

Wistfully Zulime shook her head. "Making this bed remind me of my mama."

"Remind me of mine too," Agatta added, locking eyes with Zulime.

"I used to fall for it every single time. Mama had a playful side, not Daddy though; he just had rules and more rules. Both teachers, but the more he learned the meaner he got."

"You have a sister too?" Agatta inquired.

"Sure do. Her name's Emily. She's a teacher too." Quickly, Zulime fluffed the pillows.

Grace covered the bed with a heavy old patchwork quilt. "I want to give my children sweet memories."

Furrowing her brow, "You want children?" Agatta asked.

"Umh, umh, and plenty of them. With a good husband to boot."

"I hope and pray you get them," Zulime said.

"Surely, I will."

Magdalena styled Agatta's hair in a braided chignon, leaving tresses free to tickle her ears. She held a mirror in front of her subject. "Take a gander pretty lady."

"I do believe you missed your calling."

"A masterpiece if I do say so myself." Magdalena flopped down on the bed.

Humming as she worked, Grace gathered the soiled linens and carried them downstairs to Sal. When she returned, she sat the washbowl on the floor next to the chaise.

"Up or down?" queried Zulime.

"Down." Agatta slid her gown off her shoulders; Zulime helped to roll it under her butt, then sat down beside her and removed the bandages.

Dried blood formed a gruesome palette ranging from dark red to purple to black. She lightly squeezed the sponge, dabbed it with castile soap, and cleansed the wound. It had begun to heal along its corners but the center was still very sensitive. Since Agatta didn't cringe, Zulime applied more pressure. "Still tender?"

"Not like before."

"That wench ought to be strung up."

Grace frowned. "Don't tempt me."

"I been in business seventeen years, you the first of my girls to get hurt."

"You not to blame," Agatta assured her.

"I know who to blame." Zulime covered the cut with red ocher and smeared mouton tallow along the edges. "I care about all of my girls, but it's no secret that I hold you three close to my heart."

"You know we feel the same."

"That's good to know." Zulime pinned a fresh bandage around Agatta's waist. As she helped her back into her gown, she was struck by the supple skin and lovely form. "Girl, you something else. No wonder that man is so crazy about you."

"I'm the crazy one."

"You paying for it." After pressing the back of her hand to Agatta's forehead and chest to find that she was lukewarm, Zulime rolled her sleeves down and returned to her chair.

Carrying the washbowl, Grace went downstairs while Magdalena stored away medicine. Soon both of them lay sprawled on the bed.

A peculiar though fortunate spell of silence fell over the room. Absolute. Coda. Great understanding formed in the absence of conversation. This visitation sought to give or to take, but for sure to let live.

Agatta stretched her legs out and closed her eyes briefly before resuming an idle stare. At that moment she longed for nothing. Nothing at all. It never ceased to amaze her how protected and cherished she felt in the company of her friends. Maybe because she was the youngest and most fragile thread on the loom. Though none of them were related; they were linked by God, and loved each other like blood.

Vividly, Agatta remembered Grace and Magdalena rescuing her from a cold wet alley in the quarter. Right from the start she felt at home with them. Now she felt it necessary to release her suffering from its tomb; for it needed light and her loved ones deserved to know. But in silence and darkness her sorrow had hurt so severely for so long that she was accustomed to it and her private suffering approached divine. Words seemed like trespassers. So she thought carefully about it, breathed in long and out deep and intentionally she felt the weight of her tongue between her teeth then decided to speak. But there was a distraction.

A flock of pigeons perched on the windowsill. They pecked at the shutters and fluttered their wings wildly. After capturing the women's attention they abruptly flew away.

The women settled back into repose.

Agatta spoke. "We lived on a lil' farm in Paulina. Mama and Daddy had one child—me. They used to say I was all the children God wanted them to have. Just like the sun, moon, and crops, I was enough.

"Daddy had two men working for him. Mr. Frank had worked for him since I was a baby. The other one just showed up one day, not long after New Year's in '84. He called hisself Brother Tap, but he ain't no brother of mine. Folks didn't take to him at all. He had a bad limp cause one leg was shorter than the other. He had big red eyes. So big, that even when he slept they didn't close. He was stocky built, fat really. His titties were bigger than most women's, and he drank plenty moonshine, and did the weirdest dancing you ever wanna see. Nobody knew where he came from. Folks talked that he might've run off from the crazy house or the carnival or more likely the chain gang. They shunned him too. But Paul and Addy Lugar never met a stranger; they said everybody deserved a chance, go they gave Tap one.

"Mr. Frank never took to Tap, Daddy kept him on anyhow though. Then one day, Mr. Frank came and asked for his last pay and told Daddy he couldn't work for him no more. Naturally, Daddy wanted to know why. Mr. Frank said Tap was just too strange; said he caught him naked in the barn hollering, running in circles. On top of that he was lazy—made more work than he did. Daddy was hurt, but he paid Mr. Frank and let him go on.

"After that, Daddy found hisself working harder and harder cause Tap couldn't keep his mind on nothing for long. Most he did was feed the chickens and hogs. Seem like he grumbled 'bout that. Folks kept on talking. Whenever we went to town, they warned Mama and Daddy. Told 'em how Tap would be wandering round all hours of the night, dirty, britches sagging; which was true. Even though Mama offered to wash his clothes and hem his britches, he never let her. He kept on acting strange. Drinking more, working less. Daddy put up with it a long time, but time run out like everything else."

She paused, rose up slightly on her elbows, swallowed, and reclined again. Her eyes roamed the ceiling before falling to stay on a window that may as well had looked out on Neptune.

"The last week in January, Daddy went to Empire to sell hogs and look over a plot of land. He was supposed to be gone at least six days. The whole time he was away, Tap didn't work at all. He'd come home early in the morning sloppy drunk, go to his quarters and sleep all day while me and Mama did his work. So one morning we feeding the chickens, and here come Daddy down the road, two days early. He wasn't even close to the house good fore he started to ranting 'bout where Tap was. He jumped off the wagon. Mama tried to calm him, but Daddy went straight to Tap's quarters and threw him out with no pay. Tap was mad, so mad he looked wild. Daddy ran him off. And he was gone . . . for a while.

"Late one night I heard someone beating at the door. I sat up in bed. There was a loud bang. I heard Daddy tell Mama to stay in their room. I ran out my room and hid. Tap was standing in the vestibule with a double-barrel shotgun. Mama ran after Daddy. She was holding on to him crying and pleading. Tap raised the gun, aiming at Daddy, but Mama stepped in front of him. I recollect the gun fired three times. When she fell at Daddy's feet, I ran from my hiding place. I laid cross her—I can't tell you what that look like. Daddy cried. He fought Tap hard; even had him by the neck once, but when Tap broke loose, he beat Daddy with the butt of the gun. Beat him til his head opened up. He laid there shivering in blood and tears til he went on. Tap stood over him grunting. It took him some time to notice me watching. When he did, I ran. I don't know how I got past him cause I went through the same door he came. I ran and never looked back.

"I must have wandered all night long. I never stopped moving. I don't know how far I walked. Late the next day I got hungry. Fore long I passed an orange grove and ate til I was full. I knotted a few oranges in my gown, drank water from a creek, and kept walking. Early the next morning an old man and his wife pulled up alongside me on their way to New Orleans. I rode with them. When we got here, I got out and sat in the alley."

Grace whispered in a breaking voice, "Where we found you."

"Yeah."

"How long did you sit there?" Magdalena asked.

"Not long. I reckon not even an hour."

"Child, you been through something," Zulime said.

Grace sat up. "You must've been scared."

"No, I wasn't."

"Why not?"

"The whole time I wandered, I felt like I was being led. Every time I had a need it was met. When I finally go tired, the old folks gave me a ride. And I wasn't in that alley no time fore y'all showed up. Besides, I figure I left the worst at home."

"It makes good sense when you put it that way," Grace said.

"But I'm shame cause much as I hurt, as much as I hate Tap—I never cried."

Zulime went to Agatta and embraced her. "Just cause you haven't shed water, don't mean you never cried."

# 9

## Lewd and Abandoned

For I have eaten ashes like bread, and mingled my drink with weeping.
—Psalm 102:9

Bound and determined, if Viv were still in his brothel, Sazar ascended the stairs to throw her out. He had not been there since her assault on Agatta. He wanted to give her time to leave without issue.

He opened the door to her crib to find her sprawled on the bed, swaddled under the covers asleep. After analyzing her a minute, he surveyed the room. Dusty furniture, clothing strewn every which way, empty liquor bottles littered the unswept floor. Cigar butts riddled the vanity amidst spilled toiletries. Stoically scrutinizing her room, Sazar realized that he stood in the den of a madwoman. Her space and her life were one in the same; utter discord. More disturbing, however, was that he knew things belonging to him were hidden in that mess. But he had neither the patience nor the desire to search.

Shirts, socks, underwear, and probably locks of his hair were concealed in her chaos. Talisman? Lucky charms? Whatever she called them, demented Viv believed stealing his possessions would keep him close to her. He had known other women who thought the same way, but not to this degree. Abracadabra never made me care, he concluded.

He drew the curtains, shedding further light on the disarray. Once more he scanned the room before running his hand along the headboard. He touched the deep notches in the wood; amazed by her insane ritualistic nature, which she did nothing to conceal. In fact, she flaunted it. Boldness—they had that in common. She was bold and foolish. He was bold and strategic.

She lay in a deep sleep, fatigued by booze and obsession. Slumber may well have been her only sedative. Between exhaustive puffs she snored.

Hoping that she might feel his rage and awake, he hovered above her. Much to his disappointment, she slept on and even appeared vulnerable. Her vulnerability forced him to acknowledge his role in her depravation. Loving him had taken a dreadful toll on her. They had courted, sometimes strongly. But he never took her seriously. She entered his life the way many women had, as a misguided devotee. When her affections blossomed into fanaticism with tantrums in tow, he failed to correct her. Inevitably his cavalier stance led to confusion which led to strife, and all of it backfired.

He asked himself, How many times did she get her way? If one of his other crib girls were off on female time, he couldn't take her out because Viv would pitch a bitch. Sometimes she hid the woman's shoes or blocked the door screaming.

Sazar would spend so much of the evening trying to calm her that eventually the other girl would give up on the date altogether. In return he punished Viv with a brief spell of silent treatment that she had come to expect. After a few days, he would come around. All the while she took his ambivalence for cooperation. Until tragedy altered the course.

He jerked the covers off her.

Struggling to open her sluggish eyelids, she fought the urge to fall back asleep. Lethargically, she rolled over and rubbed her tired eyes. Her tiny breasts wobbled freely, unrestrained by a partially hooked corset that she had slept in along with a petticoat and stockings. A spicy masculine odor drifted past her nostrils, almost sending her mind on an erotic tangent; but her fantasy was soon arrested. "You got to go."

His command rendered her speechless and motionless. Though she had anticipated his wrath, he still caught her off guard emotionally. Which was easy for him to do since he stocked the lion's share of her emotional storehouse. Just when she thought she felt as bad as she could, he always held the power to make her feel worse.

He opened the wardrobe, retrieved a brown Mother Hubbard and threw it to her. He ran his foot under the bed and coerced a tattered traveling bag to the middle of the floor. He emptied the wardrobe, cleaned out the dresser and vanity drawers, then stuffed as many clothes as he could into the bag. The rest he piled on the bed. Viv sat up and faced the wall.

Sazar interpreted her hesitance for insolence. "Soeur, don't tarry."

Without a word she put the dress on and found her shoes.

Puzzled by her silence he wondered, Is this defeat or pride?

Careful not to look him in the eye, Viv collected her jewelry, cosmetics, and sundries. She packed the items in a hatbox. Next she started folding her clothes.

Sighing and shrugging his shoulders, he looked on convinced that she was stalling.

To some degree she was. Her reasons, however, were worlds apart from his speculations. She had lost things: hope, him, her mind, and now a roof. Moving slowly gave her time to deal.

He went to the opposite side of the bed, pushed all of her things to the center, bundled them in the spread, and shoved it to her.

Viv slung the bundle over one shoulder, slid her bag on the other, picked up her hatbox, and went downstairs.

She was almost out the door, when Sazar leaned over the banister and called out to her. "Don't forget this," he said, dangling the silver pocket watch that she had given him.

She turned around. Though her eyes were glazed over with tears of regret, she looked right at him, "I won't," she said. She left him with a parting gift, a mystery, and the ruckus of the streets filtering past his threshold.

# 10

## Welcome To This House

*Then* will I teach transgressors thy ways; and sinners shall be converted unto thee.
—Psalm 51:13

Jovially strumming the piano, Shorty performed a high stepping tune. Wholly absorbed in the music, he rocked, tapped his feet, and bobbed his head. Of small stature, his physique halted development at puberty. But the wisdom in his eyes and gray hairs at his temples gave away his age of fifty plus years. He was an uninhibited maestro. Watching him was sheer exhilaration; his was the kind of joy that spilled over.

Curled up in a corner chair, Agatta comprised an audience of one. Her wound had almost healed completely. She was feeling much better, so she contemplated going for a walk. But on her way out, the gleeful tunes captured her ear. She enjoyed Shorty's high-stepping tunes, yet the mourning songs lured her to the parlor far more frequently. She sat patiently, knowing that he would give her what she came for.

After playing another set of spirited pieces, Shorty winked at her before winding the music down. He stretched his arms, and shifted the tempo to a brooding dirge. The low somber timbre dared to be wretched and liberating at once. Oppression was the song's muse, yet catharsis was its achievement. The sound differed from the New Orleans dirge in that its theme evolved around a poignant strain of despair. In New Orleans there was a celebration leaving the cemetery. Musicians knew this en route to the gravesite, so even the sorrow song was played with an anticipation of jubilee.

As Shorty continued to play a sub-theme of perseverance emerged. Given to reservation, Agatta resisted the summons to moan and groan; nevertheless, her spirit agreed and went through the motions. She found solace in the torrid sacredness of the arrangement. Through it she accepted that hurt and healing could coexist. "What kind of music is that?"

"Church music. In East Texas we play this at baptisms and funerals."

"I never heard nothing like it before."

"You never been to our kind of church before."

"You right. That song make me want to cry and shout at the same time."

"Back home that's what we do, my dear." Shorty swayed back, rippled his fingers over the ivory, and gave an encore.

Engrossed in the concert, Agatta closed her eyes. It was Sunday morning. She had all day long to walk.

A house *is* whatever you feel when you first set foot in it. Upon entering No. 51, Reverend

McBride discerned that it was an abode of love. Some sin, but mostly love; agape not eros. Within these walls a warmth pervaded that many *saved* homes lacked. But homes, like people, were seldom one-dimensional. Nevertheless, it was a bordello and harsh ramifications, such as violence, came with the territory of prostitution.

After reading of Agatta's attack in *The Weekly Pelican,* Luther decided to pay the women of No. 51 a visit. It was just the catalyst he needed to extend a formal invitation to the church. Though visitors were welcome anytime, special occasions were the best. The upcoming Founders' Day celebration was set for the second Sunday in May. There would be an abundance of food, fellowship, and gratitude. The congregation looked forward to praising the Lord fervently, and giving thanks for his manifold blessings upon the church. As the date approached, Luther sensed a prophetic sermon burgeoning on the horizon. In advance he prayed for lives to be changed; already he believed they would.

While waiting to be received by the hostesses, he enjoyed the hospitalities of iced tea and piano music. On impulse he tapped his feet to this familiar sound in this unfamiliar place, and blushed when he caught himself. Overall the environment proved to be a course in enlightenment. Some of his bred in the bone beliefs about brothels dissolved. Expectations of filth and rampant lasciviousness were shot down at the door.

Freshly waxed floors and polished furniture glowed like new. The sweet exotic perfume of gardenias permeated the air. Pretty curtains dressed the windows. This was one of the loveliest drawing rooms that he had ever visited.

There was a photograph album on a side table. Luther tugged at his collar then thumbed through the pictures. Judging by age, hearsay, authoritative air, and the quantity of images, he picked Zulime out from among the others. Half a dozen images captured her arm in arm with male companions. The fellows ran the gamut: old, young, sophisticated, rugged, handsome, and typical. None of them really befitted her. Luther closed the album just in time to look up and behold a presence bolder than the preview.

He stood with hat in hand when Zulime and Agatta entered the parlor. Magdalena and Grace followed them.

Agatta extended her hand. "It's good to see you again."

"The pleasure's all mine. I'm glad to see you up and about."

"I feel better everyday." Glancing over her shoulder, "I met Reverend McBride in the quarter," Agatta explained. She pointed to each of the women as she introduced them. "This is Madam Clovis. We call her Mam Zulime. Meet Magdalena Marie and Grace Lorin."

"Pleased to meet all of you."

"Likewise." Zulime shook Luther's hand. "Why don't you join us for supper?"

"Thank you kindly. Don't mind if I do."

They proceeded to the dining room, where pitchers of cold water and mint julep awaited. Sal served gumbo and hot bread for starters.

"Reverend, please say grace."

They all joined hands.

"Father, we thank you for this food. For the nourishment and strengthening of our bodies. Amen."

Every voice said, "Amen."

Slyly, Zulime inquired, "So you bring good news?"

"To tell the truth—I do." Luther paused when Zulime's attention drifted toward the portal.

"Sazar Jorda here," Sal announced.

Zulime took a sip of mint julep then smoothed out the napkin in her lap. "Show him in."

Magdalena moved down a seat while Agatta set an extra place at the table.

"Good evening all." Sazar kissed Agatta's hand, "Hello love," and eased into the seat next to her. He gave Luther a nod. "Did I luck upon a strange party or a prayer meeting?"

"Good to see you again, Mr. Jorda. A few weeks back, I read of Agatta's misfortune, so I come by to see how she faring."

Nibbling on a piece of bread, Sazar replied, "I see."

"Also my church is holding our Founders' Day celebration the second Sunday in May, May 8, to be exact." Scanning the faces gathered around the table, Luther knew that most if not all of them were Creole, and more likely to be familiar with Hail Mary than hastening to the throne or catching on fire. "I know most of you probably Catholic, and never been to a Protestant church before, but we'd be glad to have you just the same."

"My father's Catholic, but Mama converted to Baptist after the war," Zulime said. "I visited her church a few times."

"I grew up an orphan at the Sisters of the Holy Family Convent." Grace shrugged her shoulders. "I left there eleven years ago, haven't been to Mass since."

Sal returned serving a main course of smothered pork chops with roasted potatoes and mustard greens.

Agatta put small portions of everything on her plate. "I was raised Catholic but I haven't been to church since I came to New Orleans. Back home I used to like the music when we passed by your kind of church. I always wanted to go in," she said.

Magdalena slid two pork chops onto her plate. "Some of my people Catholic, some not. When I was little, one of my Pentecostal tantes took me to her church. I couldn't believe the way they sang and let the spirit move them. They praised God like he was right there."

"He was," Luther added.

Curtly, Sazar said, "I'm Catholic." He twirled his fork, "Your church welcomes all kinds of people? Strayed or saved?"

"Christ came for all."

"You know Reverend . . ."

"McBride."

"Yes. Lost souls are easy to come by. Especially in New Orleans."

"Indeed they are. But I follow the Master's lead."

"And your master just happened to lead you to a brothel housing the prettiest women in town." Sazar nudged Agatta.

"Mr. Jorda, my liking to Agatta is pure friendly relations."

"Plenty of women will befriend you."

"I know. Half of my friends are women. I do God's work; I don't question him. A man would have to be long gone blind not to see that Agatta is a beauty." Luther eyed each of the women. "They all are. Now I can see you have strong feelings for her, and I'm happy for you both. My intentions won't hinder what the two of you have."

"Why can't you just tend to the restless in your flock and let all this alone?"

"I can tend to both. A little at a time."

"As sure as sunrise, preacher man, you're just trying to make a name for yourself by redeeming a few lewd and abandoned women." Sazar leaned in, put his elbows on the table, and clasped his hands. "You're bored with liars, drunks, and thieves. Fornicators fill up the collection plate, can't get too righteous with them. Prostitutes! Aha! Missionary work in the perfect flesh. Get some loose ladies to the Lord. Some sho 'nough stars in your crown."

"People come to Christ when they're ready, not a moment sooner. If they need help understanding God's word and ways to build up their faith then I'll aid them. That's what I do. But understand, people can get to God all by themselves."

"Then let them."

"You're a pimp, but a woman can sell herself without you."

"I'm the fist, the law, the order, the overseer if you will. Yes, they can work without me, but with me they can work with peace of mind. I don't apologize for that." Except for the clinking of silverware there was silence. Sazar poured himself a glass of water then casually reared back in the chair. "You don't know the first thing about these women, let alone the lot of doxies in general. Many of them don't know a thing outside of lying on their backs. Where you think they got their first lesson? Fathers, brothers, uncles, cousins, neighbors, strangers too. From Bible breathing brothers like yourself."

"I don't just breathe it, I live it."

"Girls show up at my door, innocent as can be; except for the parts that make them women. Poor, colored, used, and forgotten. They have no one to turn to and nowhere to go."

"A lot of pain been heaped on black folks. Our women get a double portion. But only a few end up on your doorstep."

"The rest go to some other bagnio. It comes down to this, you can stand up in your pulpit stomping and hollering 'bout how you know their pain, yet you don't. And you never will."

"When I stomp and holler it's about how God knows their pain."

"I know that heartache firsthand. My mother was a whore." To no avail, Sazar searched Luther's face for any trace of shock or disbelief.

"There's more to all of us than face value. Every one of us has valleys and mountains."

"Do you know what it is to hold a woman so battered that she can't stand the touch of hands trying to help her?"

"I've held my share of broken women. And I've seen the Lord put some back together again. Many reformed prostitutes have made stalwart Christians. A few are members of my church."

"That's all fine and good Reverend, but why don't you go fish off another pier and leave my lil' part of the world alone?"

"When my work in your world is done, I'll be gone soon enough."

Sazar hunched his shoulders and ran a napkin across his mouth. "I'd prefer sooner." Tenderly, he kissed Agatta's cheek. "See you later, dolin'."

"Take care."

"Madam Clovis, thanks for a fine meal."

"Je vous en prie."

Sazar rose from his seat. "Monsieur, Mademoiselles, bonne nuit." Substance now weighed on his belly and mind. He showed himself out. As he left No. 51, he felt the tides of change surging his way. He braced himself.

# 11

## Divine Reciprocity

Be not deceived; God is not mocked: for whatsoever a man soweth that shall he also reap.
—Galatians 6:7

After Sazar threw Viv out, she rented a room at a boarding house and started looking for work. For two weeks she knocked on doors in vain. Though she boasted about her past earnings at Sazar's, proprietors repeatedly turned her away with the same response: "It's easy to make a man rich if you're willing to kill for him." Like a proverb, the statement bound itself to her conscience. She walked the streets day in and day out. Her hopes waned and calluses formed on her feet.

Her looks barred her from *sweet houses.* Being in her late twenties didn't help. She had finagled her way into Sazar's bordello, courtesy of their affair. Before then she had worked in standard brothels. Now most of those houses were full. The ones with openings didn't want troublemakers; crossing Sazar had virtually blackballed her.

On a rainy muggy Saturday evening she resolved to go where hopeless whores went, to a cathouse. The lowest rank of assignation houses. With her hand sore and red from clenching an umbrella for hours, she treaded her way to a dilapidated block of Rampart. Red lanterns flickered on all the porches. Because it was three stories, and probably had room for more girls, she chose the narrow lopsided shingle house with severely chipped pink paint and broken windows. True to her nature, she gravitated toward that which was on a shaky foundation.

"I'm so tired of looking," she whispered to herself and knocked on the door.

A skinny Negro woman under a wild mane of kinky white hair answered. Shuffling a cigarette between her lips, she looked Viv up and down. "Moochie lookin' for girls." She stepped aside. "Come in."

Viv entered the sphere of ruins. Every piece of rickety furniture in sight had torn upholstery. Faded curtains harbored moths. Roaches crawled the floors and walls in teams. A rotten odor hung in the air.

"What's your name precious?"

"Viv. Yours?"

"Luscious Liz. Follow me."

As they neared the rear of the house, the foul smell of human flesh intensified. Viv stopped when Liz went behind the staircase. "Back here," she called and opened the door.

Reluctantly, Viv followed. Nauseated by the stench, she feared fainting. She peeked inside the small room, and almost gasped at the mass of mortal flesh stationed on a freestanding mattress.

Moochie weighed around six hundred pounds on a four and a half foot frame. Thus, she was completely bedridden. With the help of thirteen live-in girls, she ran the business.

Though Viv avoided eye contact, and pretended not to see the mice circling the mattress; she still came face to face with the wages of sin. Hers was lust; gluttony was Moochie's offence. After unraveling their lives, sin cast them into the pit of strumpet hell.

"Moochie, this Viv. She lookin' for work."

Trying hard to conceal her disgust, Viv forced a smile. "Pleased to meet you," she said, from the doorway.

In the midst of wheezing, Moochie nodded then finally uttered something.

"Pardon?"

"She'll take you," Liz clarified.

"Thank you." Viv backed away.

Liz closed the door to Moochie's room. "Tips are yours to keep. Charge at least three dollars a john. More, if you can get it. Pay her half of every day's earnings. You can bunk with—"

"I have a place to stay. I just need work."

"Fine. You can use any empty crib. You gon' start tonight?"

"No. Tomorrow's fine." Using all of her energy to hold her breath against the stench, Viv practically ran out of the house. I can't work here long, she thought.

More and more the notion of a better or at least different life consumed Viv. Although she had not figured out any definite plans, the very possibility was a welcome diversion. Somewhere in the sequence she had a epiphany: her life had to be about more than loving Sazar Jorda because thus far that was a tremendous waste of time.

She had a routine. After work, she went straight home to the quaint room that she rented on St. Philip in Tremé. Abby remained her closest friend; they got together at least once a week.

Viv kept her colleagues at arm's length. She greeted Moochie from the hall, and paid her by passing the money to whomever was nearby. Her conversation with the boss was limited to "hello" and "see you tomorrow." Whether she was dipping snuff, devouring whole chickens, or loading up the bedpan; she made Viv's stomach turn.

On top of that, Viv couldn't decipher her speech. Moochie grunted and made wild gestures, pointing and waving sporadically at people, places, and things. Then suddenly she would break into riotous laughter, only to have it impeded by severe coughing. Someone would rush to pat her on the back, or bring her water. When she regained her composure, she would resume laughing, some of the girls laughed with her, pretending to understand her humor.

About every ten days or so, four of the staff teamed up to bathe Moochie. Two of them moved flesh while the other pair washed and rinsed. Her butt often had its share of puss-running bedsores. The women treated them with hot lard. Then there was the task of washing and combing her wig. No matter what they did, it sat on her head crooked, and looked like a damn raccoon.

Operating with few restrictions, the house had strayed far from merely being loose. Residents could walk around naked and sleep wherever the inclination to do so found them. If there was a hot meal, they grabbed the nearest piece of silverware and ate right out of the pot.

Most of the women had ludicrous tags like Mellow Melissa, Easy Esther, and Sugar Baby. Titles that were supposed to make them more alluring. Ranging from twelve years old to late sixties, hard living had branded their bodies with blemishes, scars, and wrinkles. Many were snaggletooth. Their patrons were either drunk, broke, desperate, or liked slumming; most were all of the above.

After they learned of Viv's past exploits, they tried calling her "Vicious Viv," but she shrugged them off, and put up an emotional barricade. She suffered from her own brand of madness. She could not afford to contract theirs.

By nightfall Moochie's went from cathouse to haunted house. Doors slammed constantly. Wild eerie laughter squealed from every corner of the leaning shack. Folks restlessly trafficked up and down the creaking stairs.

Viv tuned out the chaos, and ventured to the parlor to size up prospects, hoping for something other than the usual slew of barefoot vagabonds.

Liz sat by the door puffing on a cigarette, and staring at her feet while ashes landed in her lap.

Viv joined Melissa and Esther, who stood against the wall. The three of them served as a passive audience watching a couple of girls dance with an elderly humpbacked man wearing long johns. They tossed his trousers to and fro as he crouched down, bluffing to crawl between their legs. When he tired of that exercise, the girls took him to a crib.

Lost in thought Viv almost missed Liz abruptly springing to her feet to answer the door. A young man entered. He twiddled his thumbs. His clothes were too big for him. A foul smelling cigar protruded from his lips.

Liz welcomed him. "Hi dere, sugar."

"Ah . . . I . . . I . . . I . . ." he stuttered. Bowing his head, he blurted out, "Come to get a girl."

Melissa came forward. "You got one." She led him off.

Viv was about to look away when another man stepped inside.

A slouch hat cocked to one side partially concealed his face. He wore a dark grey custom suit and a scarf tie. The moonlight cast a sparkle on his sterling cufflinks. His boots boasted a fresh spit shine. He didn't limp, but he carried a walking stick. An odd one, it had a falcon crest.

Cloaked behind Liz's thick haze of smoke, he appeared as an apparition. So Viv stepped into the light to take stock of him.

Immediately she saw that his face was not really a face, but a horrid maze of scars. Some of the keloids on his forehead had jagged tears. Scars, white and waxy, marred his cheeks and nose. His lips attested to minor damage; compared to the rest of his face they were relatively intact. Judging by his unscathed skin, his natural coloring was pecan-brown.

By the confidence of his stride, Viv figured he must have been a handsome man once. It's a shame to look at someone and see who they used to be.

He averted his gaze to the floor, his cane, and Esther's hips. Yet Viv was certain that he noticed her.

"What's your pleasure?" Liz asked.

"A woman."

"How 'bout me?" Esther smiled and strutted toward him.

"No. She'll do," he said, pointing to Viv.

"Hey girl! You got one." Esther called out.

Viv smiled at him then swaggered upstairs. Winding her hips seductively, she paced herself so that he could keep up with her, inhale her scent, and study her form, but not touch her. She felt him sizing her up the way a farmer would livestock. She opened the door to a damp crib. The hypnotic sweet odor of opium enveloped them. "Wanna leave the door cracked?"

"No."

"What's your name?"

"Does it matter?"

"Umh, it's always nice to know. Mine's Viv." Nervously, she glanced around the room, waiting for his cue regarding where and how she should position herself.

As quickly as he could have snapped his fingers, he tapped the cane on the hardwoods. "Floor."

She squatted down, spread her legs, and leaned back on her palms.

With a sinister smirk planted on his face, he casually twirled the cane then lightly poked it in her crouch. She giggled. Next he locked the door, and dropped the key in his coat pocket.

"What you do that for?"

"Privacy."

"Round here everybody mind they own business."

In a bizarre vaudeville fashion, he juggled the cane then swung it behind him. At least four times he did this. By now the smirk had vanished. Finally, he went back to Viv, and ran the cane under her skirt. Wielding greater force, he poked her in the crouch again.

Faking a smile, she went along with the play. Out of curiosity, and a lack of interesting objects, she focused on his face.

"Alistar," he said, swooping down so that they were momentarily up close.

"Huh?" Viv jumped.

"You wanted to know my name."

She placed her hand across her racing heart, hoping that contact might calm it.

Unabashedly, Alistar allowed her to stare at his face. "Ugly?"

"Accident?"

"No."

"On purpose?"

"Yes."

"You must have made somebody awfully mad."

"Nobody got the right to get this mad." Alistar touched his face as though he were handling a foreign object—a fragile one.

"Some folks do."

"You been this mad?"

"Sure have." Now she sat with her knees bent and her arms wrapped around them, coquettishly rocking back and forth.

He studied her. There she was, another shape-shifting minx able to revamp in the twinkle of an eye from a sadist to a helpless little girl. A woman's demeanor is her hustle; he wondered why he hadn't realized that before.

Jahla Dupree was her name. Alistar Kahn, a handsome cabinetmaker, had his choice of prospects. But his heart belonged to her. Although she was as fleeting as a sparrow, he pursued her under the persuasion that love conquers all.

After one visit with the comely petite, auburn haired Cyprian, he became a regular. Her caramel-colored skin was soft to his touch. Perpetually he longed to stare into her bewitching hazel eyes. She was sly and self-assured, which he liked. She told dirty jokes without blushing. Her laughter was wild and sounded like the confusing babel of unknown tongues.

Yet even when he held her with unguarded tenderness, there existed a wall of partition between them—business. Money secured her company, so communication was awkward. While he tried to discuss the rewards of commitment, she whispered sweet nothings and prodded him for material things.

Frequently he had asked to be her beau, and she casually rejected him. Still, he visited her every Wednesday for six months, showering her with gifts and a handsome fee. Alistar resolved that a little Jahla was better than no Jahla at all.

On a hot July hump day after soaking wet playful sex, they rested. As a fly circled the window and a vendor rang a triangle peddling pork chops, he asked for her hand in marriage. Nonchalantly, she consented.

Two days later they were married at St. Louis Cathedral. Alistar's brother and sister-in-law witnessed the ceremony. In pristine white, Jahla looked angelic. Her sins found loopholes through the eyelets of her veil. A bouquet of pink roses perfumed her past. With conviction she looked Alistar in the eyes and said, "I do."

For nearly a year they enjoyed blissful matrimony. She exceeded his expectations of a good wife. She kept their Tremé house immaculate, and prepared her husband's meals with time and care. Her feasts so delighted him that he often compared them to his mother's. They went out for dinner and dancing regularly. Pretty Jahla looked swell on Alistar's arm; his ego blossomed when other men admired her.

Marriage became an ever-expanding paradise for him. Filled with companionship, joy, and a lovemaking horn of plenty. Every now and then if she were abrupt, or her eyes wandered, or her "I love you's" lacked depth, he dismissed the behavior as typical female moodiness.

He could not read her mind. So unbeknownst to him, she missed her old life. She longed for smoke filled barrooms and hoodlum spontaneity. She preferred drifting asleep as the cock crowed instead of rolling over to Mr. Predictable, and going par for the course of mundane domesticity. More than anything, she wanted to consume the thoughts of other men again.

A letter from Sabo, a former beau, had triggered her unrest. She started seeing him again. Their liaisons occurred during the day while Alistar worked. She covered her tracks by tidying up the house as soon as Alistar left for the day. Early in the morning while supper pots simmered, she made the bed, swept, mopped, and dusted. She could see Sabo any day, Tuesday through Friday; Monday was washday. After dinner was done and the house in order, she would meet Sabo, and they went about their clandestine affair. Strategically she arrived home before her husband. Careful not to rouse his suspicion; when he walked through the door she was sure to be engaged in some noble task: stirring a pot, setting the table, or sewing a button on one of his shirts.

She satisfied her worldly appetite and kept the home calm until Sabo got greedy. He wanted her to be less wife and more flame. Preferring his strong arm to her husband's gentle touch, she arranged her schedule to oblige him. Eventually, Sabo's time slipped into Alistar's.

It didn't happen often at first. But a few times Alistar came home to a lonely house. He grew suspicious and doubt chipped away at his trust. When Jahla returned her excuse was always the same: she was visiting old friends and lost track of time. He held his piece. However, he knew better. Her clothing was much too suggestive for platonic company. On each occasion her hair had been disheveled and the damnest heat surrounded her. After a weak explanation, she quickly retreated to bed, complained of a headache, and fell fast asleep.

Then she began to come home late more often. Once she stayed gone for an entire weekend and came home to a heated confrontation. During which Alistar reminded her of how much he had done for her, and how much he had sacrificed. So she swung back into the devoted wife routine.

Things operated smoothly again. So one evening after dinner while he read and she washed dishes, Jahla asked if she could visit Rachel, a friend sick with pleurisy. Though she had never mentioned this friend before, he consented. Since it was dark out, he offered to escort her. But she assured him that Rachel lived nearby on St. Louis, and then poured him a brandy. She kissed his hand, grabbed her shawl and purse and left.

He waited a few minutes then followed her.

In plain sight, she walked two blocks ahead of him. Braving the chilly October air, with folded arms she walked briskly. She passed St. Louis and continued to Conti, and went into Dracon's.

Through the swinging doors Alistar watched her.

She greeted acquaintances before going upstairs to the third story.

Alistar entered the saloon and pursued her. His heart sank as he witnessed her transforming into her old self. Siren. Gliding effortlessly, shoulders arched back, head slanted upward as allegiant chandeliers dappled light on her face. Grinning flirtatiously, exuding the confidence, independence, and bewitching charm that first caught his eye.

She went to the end of the hall. She moved so quickly through the loiterers that Alistar lost sight of her. He heard knocking. Next he saw her disappear behind a closing door. His head grew hot. Hurrying, he almost fell.

He turned the knob of a locked door, so he had to knock. "Jahla come out!" He had to knock again and even harder.

She peeked out. "Why you come here?" Her voice reverted to its old slur.

"Come home."

"I think about it."

"Think? We're married."

"Go, please." She backed away, and tried to close the door, but he pushed his way in. She stumbled backwards as the door slammed against the wall.

Stunned, Alistar stopped short of the threshold.

Resting on a cot was Sabo, decked out in a brown suit, a yellow silk cravat, and a wide-brimmed hat. He projected all the flair and cockiness of a man who lived on the fringes of society. "Straighten this out. I be back in a minute."

"Well—wait," she said. He was gone before she could think of anything else to say. Embarrassed by Sabo's lack of interest, she said to Alistar, "I'm staying here."

"I love you."

"I don't need your love."

"Come!" He grabbed her arm.

"No!" She pulled away. Her shawl fell to the floor.

"Don't do this. Remember your vows."

"I do. Day in, day out, same old thing. Cooking, cleaning, you."

"You chose to wed me."

"It was just something to do. Now it don't suit me."

"It would if you let it."

"Leave me now. Maybe I think it over."

Desperate and left with nothing more to say, he endeavored to carry her off despite her kicking and hissing. Then in a fit of rage, she slapped him and broke free.

Though the pain from her blow was no more than a brief sting, she angered him greatly. He refrained for a moment. Then fury pushed love into the shadows, he lunged at her, and clenched her neck.

"Let me go! I don't want you!" She bucked, but he held fast, coercing her toward the door. Gasping for air, she exerted enough strength to hoist her tiny foot, kicked him in the groin, and freed herself.

Wailing in pain, Alistar fell onto the cot. Jahla frantically searched for her purse. It was on the night table next to the lamp. As she reached for it, he struck her across the back. Disoriented, she reached for the purse again. He seized her hand. “Bastard! Turn me loose! I never loved you!”

They struggled. Positioning himself to throw her over his shoulder, he went for her waist. With her hands free, she quickly maneuvered to seize the lamp, and bashed it into his forehead. The shattered glass liberated a flaming wick. His face, now bathed in kerosene, ignited. He crumbled to floor, screaming like a tortured madman.

She grabbed her purse and fled.

In agony and darkness, Alistar crawled about haphazardly as the flames ravaged his identity. His frightened hands made rushed futile attempts to quench the flames, but the fire parched his fingers. Searching for an exit, he groped in the dark, sickened by the smell of his burning hair and skin. His hands became tangled in a cloth. Hastily, he bundled it and covered his face. When his seared flesh peeled off onto Jahla’s shawl leaving a mask of raw tissue, he wept like no tomorrow. He tried to stand, but collapsed under pain that left him weak and dizzy. Groaning, he dragged himself out to the balcony. Peering through the rails, he cried a harrowing cry, “Help me!”

Alistar’s audible awareness amplified to incalculable dimensions. Everything he heard comprised his haunting vault. The music stopped. Conversations hushed. Glasses, bottles, and chips hit the tables sounding like a suite of castanets. Cards fell in a ripple. The most diabolical sound of all: the flight of his beloved transgressor. Panting, running, *swoosh* through the swinging doors, and the hellhound was gone.

Left behind, Alistar survived his first set of spectators. He detected stares from two bottomless wells: pity and horror. He would come to realize that every scrutinizing leer would puncture his spirit as deeply as the one before.

Meddling the cane between Viv's legs failed to produce the response that Alistar desired. He had hoped she would feign arousal. Instead she focused on his grotesque face, eyeballing him with overt curiosity, and not one trace of sympathy. She watched him with a fascination normally reserved for lynchings and hurricanes.

He did not find her particularly appealing. Initially, her freckles signaled that she might be funny or even friendly; thus far, she was neither. After drawing a blank when he tried to imagine what she looked like copulating, he concluded that false sincerity was not part of her repertoire. Which was fine, since her brazenness would make things easier.

One redemptive quality on her part could have swayed him. His emotions were unstaid. Sometimes he wanted blood; other times he wanted compassion. But in Viv, he found a Jahla-symbol—a coldhearted jade.

Roving the cane under her skirt, he asked, "That don't bother you?"

"Nope."

He drew back then rammed the stick into her sex. "Ouch!" she screamed. Pain blazed from her slit to her pelvis. Scooting back on her elbows, she called, "Somebody help!" But noise sank her plea.

"You been this mad?"

"I didn't mean no harm." She eased away, planting herself in a corner. "Please don't."

Twirling his cruel baton, he swatted her left side. With a single blow he struck her shoulder, her face, and busted her lip. "Now you got good reason to get this mad." He burst into insane laughter then batted her head and kicked her in the stomach.

Her equilibrium faltered under the torture. The pangs in her skull obliterated her thoughts as she fought to stay conscious. Drooling blood and spit, she toppled over in a fetal position. Alistar's foot had hurled Medusa into the pit of her belly, loosing a slew of serpents to gnaw at her intestines in their quest for the light of day.

"Roll over," he said, poking his foot at her thigh, "on your face."

Shifting her weight seemed as plausible as moving a mountain, but fear coerced her to obey. She pressed her nose to the damp floor, and licked her swelling bloody lip.

He stooped down, raised her skirt up, and pulled her drawers down. Then he fiddled the cane between her buttocks. Now his britches stiffened.

"No . . . no . . . no more."

"You mad?" he whispered.

Trepidation rendered her silent. She listened as he paced the floor. Suddenly, he stopped. Maybe he gone, she thought. Her eyelids flickered. Despite straining to focus, her vision remained extremely blurred. As darkness slipped over her, staying alert became an obsession. She feared that if she passed out, she would never wake. Hesitantly, she coughed up the spoonful of blood that she had collected on her tongue. The taste of life assured her that she was still alive. She sighed, thinking she might survive. But her faith was soon shaken, when out of nowhere Alistar's shadow surfaced. Then the diabolical steps. Though obscured, she saw the shiny boots progressing toward her. Dread banished all hope.

Cane in hand, he slowly tauntingly stroked her spine. He moaned. She whimpered. Now his libido quickened. "How can a whore be proud?" Again he stroked her spine. "You hear me?"

Viv lay motionless and speechless. "You one of them strong bitches." The climax of his fury came with him vehemently rapping the cane across her back again and again. He got a higher high every time her ribs cracked. After the sixth blow he rested, surveyed his damage, sucked his teeth. While she convulsed and whined, he stored her contortions in his memory. He contemplated stomping her; however, for no particular reason, he did not. So he propped his foot on her neck and spat on her.

Casually twirling his cane, he puckered his lips as though he were about to whistle; instead he just blew. Emptiness and sorrow resumed their places within him. Allotting Viv a stay in his hell only deepened his pit. He glanced at her one last time, and regretted ever having set foot in any whorehouses. Why we treat each other so bad? he asked himself. He unlocked the door, tossed the key, and left.

Viv saw the key fall near her elbow. Maybe he really was gone this time. Now she could call for help. Elevating her head an inch off the floor, she mobilized what she thought was strength. She lifted her tongue slightly. An injured jaw offered sufficient leverage to part her lips. Yet the same as any nightmare, a whiff of air escaped and darkness cascaded over her. Her chin landed in a shallow ruby pool.

# 12

## Sick and Shut In

Leave there thy gift before the altar, and go thy way; first be reconciled to thy brother, and then come and offer thy gift.

—Matthew 5:24

The only thing that troubled Sazar more than a victimized woman was having a hand in her suffering, directly or indirectly. Since his teens he had jilted numerous women, so he dealt easily with their anger and spite. Because rejection usually wasn't life threatening, he counted it as a hazard of romance. A physical assault, however, was entirely different. By way of a peculiar scheme of incidents, he had involuntarily violated his longstanding credo: I shall not suffer a woman. In a matter of weeks, he had found himself inadvertently responsible for the bodily harm of two.

When he learned from Abby that Viv had been attacked, it struck him as odd that he should care at all. Then he realized, whereas Viv had over appraised the sexual aspect of their relationship, he had valued their camaraderie. Though he still held a tinge of anger toward her for hurting Agatta, Agatta was practically healed and greatly loved.

Outside of his will, he was genuinely concerned about Viv. He could not fully understand why he felt the need to visit her. Maybe because they shared a peculiar history? Whatever the reason, he wanted to reconcile.

As he walked up Tulane Avenue, the closer he came to Charity Hospital the more anxious he grew to make amends. Even the name of the place evoked compassion and compelled him to set things right. For over a hundred and fifty years, Charity had doled out free care to the multitudes of ill, injured, and infirmed. All he had to do was show mercy to one. By the time he made it to the hospital, he no longer needed to understand his being there.

The vestibule served as a way station for those awaiting care. Falls, poisonings, shootings, stabbings, beatings, insanity, pneumonia, cholera, and syphilis created an onslaught of patients.

A young nun greeted Sazar and led him upstairs to the second of the hospital's three stories. She guided him down the corridor to the colored female ward. "There's Miss Monroe, in the last bed." The nun pointed to the left.

"Merci beaucoup." Sazar went to the end of the ward.

A stark white wall served as a canvas for Viv to project images of a new life. While she recuperated from a concussion, six fractured ribs, a busted lip, and a host of black and blue, she imagined a life far removed from prostitution. A life away from New Orleans. A life without Sazar Jorda. Daily the nuns prayed for her, assured her that she was fortunate, and that God was not through with her. All very well intended consolations, but she still had her fair share of questions. In the meantime, she hoped that the burdens of uncertainty and loneliness would disappear with the black and blue. In the meantime she would come up with a plan. She contemplated going home to Thibodeaux. But right now she needed to rest. Under the influence of laudanum she was drowsy, and her subconscious blossomed with visions of well-stocked pantries, fat laughing babies, and strong bare-chested men galloping out the ocean on war painted stallions.

Sazar pulled a chair next to her bed. “You awake?”

“I must be dead or dreaming.”

“Non. Comment ça va?”

“I’m still here. Is that why you come? To see if this bed be my cooling board?”

“I don’t know why I came. Before I could change my mind, I was here.”

“Serve me right, huh?”

“Your misfortune brings me no joy and I regret my part in it.”

“Cher, you didn’t do this.”

“I should have set some boundaries, made things clear.”

“You never asked me to love you. Nothing could’ve stopped me.”

“Wish you could turn around?”

“No.” She took his hand and traced the lines in his palm. “If I could have, I would have loved you more. Matters a damn that you not good for me.”

"You won't feel that way forever."

"You come by here to share that?"

"I came by here to see you, and tell you that I don't wish to be liable for any woman's suffering. Here lately—"

"We got our own will."

"I know. But you frail in some places, and tender in others. I need to be more careful."

"You will be. She know you here?"

"No. She may not know you're here."

"News travels fast. Knowing her, she won't mind."

"That's Agatta alright."

"I caused you both a lot of grief."

"We hold nothing against you." He leaned closer to her. "I don't have the right to and Agatta doesn't have a bitter bone in her body."

"I'm paying big for all the trouble I caused."

"We always seem to be paying for something." He eased back and watched her eyelids grow heavy.

She couldn't help succumbing to sleep. She nestled her face in the pillow, and started dozing off.

As easily as peeling a soft tangerine, one by one he freed his fingers from hers. He was glad that they were able to sever ties graciously and for the greater good—the rest of their lives. "I'll go now. You get some rest."

Through her barely opened eyes she saw him retreating. Undeniably, he was and would perhaps forever be the most beautiful creature she ever beheld. "Sazar."

"Oui."

"The time to rescue a woman is before she falls." Viv eased the stiff sheet over her shoulders and closed her eyes. Hearing the brevity and clarity of his departure, she relished their first sane encounter.

# 13

## Truth

These *are* the things that ye shall do; Speak ye every man the truth to his neighbour; execute the judgment of truth and peace in your gates.
—Zechariah 8:16

Grace stared out the window at a small boy who had tripped over his shoelace and fallen. His mother spat on a handkerchief and wiped his bruised knee then she kissed him and mussed up his hair. The child restrained his tears and forced a smile. No wonder some people weep buckets and faint at their mama's gravesite, Grace thought. Mother and child held her captive and stirred the desire to have children of her own someday.

She yearned to drip life into them from her breasts. She longed to assuage their fears. She wanted to gather them around a warm hearth and tell tales that would excite their imaginations. She planned to whisper truth into their tiny ears to instruct them and build them up. She could hardly wait to let them know that while life may present numerous mysteries, their mama's love was sure and constant. She would count it a privilege to teach them to love one another and to know that kind of love only existed at home. Yes, she thought, no wonder.

Saturday mornings were typically slow enough to partake in daydreaming, not at all like bustling Saturday nights. Though there were other girls in the parlor to keep her company, Grace would have rather been in the kitchen gossiping with Magdalena and Agatta over a hot cup of chickory coffee with too much sugar in it.

Zulime cleared her throat as she escorted two young men into the parlor. They wore loose fitting dungarees and new brown boots. Their faces were sun-parched and their hair looked like straw. One was about six feet tall, the other a foot shorter; otherwise they looked like brothers. "Gentlemen, look around and find a lady who suits your fancy. We have Bridgitte," who sat on the sofa and winked. "There's Miss Valerie," who leaned on the piano and waved. "Maybe you like Grace," who cut her eyes away from the men as they grinned at her, leaving them to wish she had a willing twin. "Well gentlemen, who's your pleasure?"

The shorter one pulled his ear and looked Grace over again as she smugly turned away. With his libido in an uproar he made peace with a pleasing though less favored option, he pointed to Bridgitte. Twisting her hair, she smiled showing off the dimples etched in her cheeks. Then she giggled the giggle of a lascivious scoundrel. She wiggled her bare alabaster toes. Her parabola-shaped feet were an aphrodisiac in their own right, it was plausible to believe that they had been bound in silk and seldom touched the ground. Her feet were often kissed and caressed by strangers, suitors, and customers alike. “We gon’ have a swell time,” she said, locking arms with her john.

“I’m sure we will,” he replied.

The tall one chose Valerie, a brown-skinned girl with short tight curly hair and big kind eyes. She kept an expression that hinted she was about to smile, but decided not to follow through. As placid as a Greek statue, her long chin pointed upward while she reveled in some clandestine knowledge. Today, she was clothed in a peach-colored frock; the sort of attire that Zulime loathed. However, Valerie’s mode of dress did not ward off customers, so the boss held her peace. With her hip pressed to the piano, she took time approaching her caller, extending one leg then slowly bringing the other forward. Finally she asked, “How do you do?”

The tall man was at a loss for words and perspiring.

“Fellas, I trust you’ll have a fine time.” Zulime saw the four of them out before turning her attention to Grace, who now appeared to be oblivious to her surroundings.

To her mind’s melody, Grace calmly rocked from side to side.

“Miss Lorin!” Zulime called.

“Mam?”

“You’re free to say when you want the day off.”

“I know.”

“Good. Next time, don’t put on that kind of show.”

“Yes Mam.”

"Morning ladies." Agatta took a seat and sat a comb and brush in her lap.

Magdalena followed slinging wet hair away from her face and shoulders. "Whew! How y'all feeling?" She gave a vial of coconut oil and hairpins to Agatta then sat on the floor between her knees. "Leave the back down."

"Hold you head right. I want it to be neat." Agatta combed Magdalena's hair in long even strokes, and rubbed oil into her scalp.

"I thought y'all went out," Zulime said, taking a seat. "I didn't see you at all earlier."

"Probably cause it took them all morning to wash Mag's hair," Grace added.

Parting the damp hair down the middle, Agatta said, "It felt like all morning."

"When I was little, Ma Dear used to wash my hair and put it in one plait. It would take two days to dry. Then I would take it down and fix it like I wanted."

"Hold you head straight and I'll fix it like you want."

"Leave the back hanging."

"I heard you the first time."

Zulime asked. "How in the world you two ever accomplish anything?"

"Barely, cause this girl wants everything just so," Magdalena answered. "But I reckon her stylish ways have benefits, seeing as how she got Jorda to where he can't see nothing else."

"I don't see nothing else either." Meticulously, Agatta twisted Magdalena's tresses on each side, and pinned it just past her ears, leaving the back to fall freely. She teased the loose strands a little before putting the comb aside. "Go look."

Magdalena went to the mirror above the fireplace, sashayed, and held the loose hair up to watch it cascade over her shoulders. "My, my, my. It takes a special talent to turn a harlot into an angel."

"Thank you my lady, but I'm too tired to take a bow."

"Both of you crazy," Zulime chuckled.

Grace tapped her nails on the windowsill. "If you had the energy, you could take two."

"For what?" Agatta asked.

"You the only woman I ever known to get revenge without having to lift a finger." Grace went over and scooted next to Agatta. "Viv got hold to a cruel prospect."

"What you say?" Magdalena gasped.

"She was down there working in some shack on Rampart; supposedly the one that big fat woman run. The one so big she can't walk."

With a hand on her forehead, Magdalena tried to recall the proprietor's name. "I know . . . umh? Her name won't come to mind right now."

"Moochie," Zulime said.

"Yeah. Anyway, some rogue damn near beat her to death with a cane. She laid up at Charity."

"God don't sleep," sighed Zulime. "Will she live?"

"They say she'll heal, but her sporting days over."

In a single swoop Zulime spread an Oriental fan with a casualness usually reserved for the front porch. "She probably scared to death of men now."

"All of us ought to be scared of them," Agatta said.

"No, no, no! Mam is careful," implored Magdalena. She folded her skirt between her thighs and sat on the arm of a sofa. "Besides, the fee keeps that sort out of here. And she got her share of pistols and a shotgun."

"But if she can't get to one in time, it's just like she got none."

"Mam's never had a girl to get hurt."

"Never have don't mean never will."

"Agatta, you worry too much. It ain't hardly likely. Mam's got the law in her pocket and frequently in her beds. The wrong sort know better than to roughhouse sweet house stock."

"The law lets her run this house, they don't say nothing about protecting us."

"Lucky for us, mostly the well-to-do frequent here. Nothing like that could ever happen under this roof."

"A rich man can slaughter a whore just a easy as a poor man. Inside this house or out. We're whores. Black whores. Whether we wear French lace or sackcloth, our lives don't count for much in the eyes of the law. Everyday that we wake up in one piece, luck has more to do with it than anything else. Every time you turn a corner or cross the street or hear footsteps behind you, you got to wonder if you in harm's way. Any of us could lose our lives cause some loon knows what we do and don't like it." Agatta wiped oil off her hands with a handkerchief. "We have to watch those we know and those we don't."

Magdalena slapped her thigh. "Whew child! You don't have much faith in men. How did Jorda ever get close to you?"

"Slow and easy."

"That's the best way," Zulime added, toying with the huge emerald that graced her bosom.

"Hah!" Agatta exclaimed. "How did old Numa woo you? Did he drop two tablespoons of batty in your cocktail?"

"There, there, stormy. I was batty when he met me."

Immanuel Tabernacle sat on the north end of Robertson Street. A modest white structure with red brick steps and a cast-iron steeple. The doors were open. A basin of soapy water sat in the vestibule. Inside three women were engrossed in rigorous cleaning. One dusted the pews, another mopped the isles, and one washed the windows.

Agatta looked on, amazed at their contentment. The woman labored as though their tasks gave them the greatest peace to be had. Undetected she left them to their work, and walked behind the sanctuary to a smaller annex.

Laughing voices, masculine and feminine filtered from the building. Though unable to determine if Luther's voice were among them, she hoped to find him there. She passed a group of small girls playing hopscotch. They took an intermission to study her and then resumed their game.

An aroma of baked cinnamon and sugar hung over the porch. Agatta suspected that hot apple pie was the culprit. It had been a long time since she bit a crust that melted in her mouth. She approached the entrance when Luther emerged and welcomed her. “Good evening, lady,” he said, taking her by both hands.

“Hello Reverend.”

“You doing alright.”

“I won’t complain.”

“That’s wise, cause it never does any good. Come on in.”

An old man spread white cloth over each of the four large rectangular dining tables inside the fellowship hall. A single pew ran the length of the East wall, the only wall with windows. Two women wearing aprons and kerchiefs placed hot pies and cakes on the serving table outside the kitchen. Steam had moistened their skins and given their middle-aged faces a youthful sheen.

“Y’all this Miss Agatta,” Luther said. “That’s Deacon Tyler, Sister Davis, and Sister Maxwell.”

“Help yourself to something sweet before you go,” Sister Davis offered.

“Thank you kindly.”

Luther invited Agatta to take a seat on the pew then sat down beside her. “I’m so glad you decided to stop by.”

“I wanted to see it for myself.” Hoping that bliss would not betray her and make her look foolish, Agatta tried to conceal the childlike awe and euphoria that she felt. "So this is your church," she said, looking around, imagining what it must be like on Sundays.

"It's the Lord's church, we just watching it for him."

"It's something alright . . . this place, these people."

"Nothing like the Master's work."

"I see."

"It wasn't always like this; the building out front is new. We razed the old church and built the one you see there now. The old church was small, but for a long time it was all we needed. Slowly but surely our congregation grew, new people, growing families."

"Now here you are."

"Here we are. Proof of what God can do."

"Can God fix people?"

"They're his specialty."

"I reckon I need fixing."

"We all do in one way or another."

Her shoulders sank. "I can't stand this way of life much longer."

"You don't have to."

"I never saw my life coming to this. Now it's hard to see my way out. My life is peculiar. Sometimes I feel like the richest woman in the world, then I see my lot for what it really is and I know better."

"Most people I know have those same feelings at some point. There are days when I feel that I have everything I need or could ever want. Then I think down the road and my everything won't do. Those are the times that I'm reminded, 'For what shall it profit a man, if he shall gain the whole world, and lose his own soul?' "

"What does it profit a woman to lose both?"

"This been on your mind for awhile."

"Lately, all the time."

"You pray on it?"

"I don't pray."

"You prayed as a child?"

"My childhood been gone."

"But you do remember that prayer is a conversation with God, where we tell him our hurts, our fears, and ask for his help?"

Agatta recalled her last prayer, *God please help Daddy*. "Not all prayers are answered."

"Our prayers may not be answered the way we want, but we have the assurance of knowing that the Lord hears all prayers."

"Even a harlot's."

"Absolutely."

"What does he do after he listens?"

"His will."

"What if his will ain't mine? What if his will hurt me?"

"Then ask him to heal your hurt, and to help you accept his will."

"That's easy for you to say because you haven't had to accept evil as God's will."

"Agatta, the evils that I've had to accept may be different from yours but I, like you, have to understand that we live in a fallen world. As a result we will face evil."

"Where is God when we face evil?"

"The same place he was when his son was on the cross."

"But look what evil did to me."

"God can heal you. Give him your burdens and ask him to give you rest."

"That's easier said than done."

"Try and trust. That's all God asks. Sister, we don't get all the answers on this side."

"Somehow, I figured that much."

"Good, real good."

Agatta rose to leave. "Thank you."

"You're most welcome. These doors are always open."

# 14

## Founders' Day

Preach the word; be instant in season, out of season; reprove, rebuke, exhort with all longsuffering and doctrine.

—2 Timothy 4:2

A somber grey sky cradled morning. Yet the old folks said they didn't smell rain, and the old folks were never wrong. Doubters, however, feared the clouds would burst into tears and turn buckets of potato salad into sludge.

Rain or none, nothing dampened spirits at Immanuel Tabernacle. At the last minute the deacons thought it might be nice to dine outdoors; the way they had in the old days. The members obliged and the picnic tables were sat out on the lawn. Another spur of the moment decision was to feast before the message. Feast they did. They ate fried chicken, buttered rolls, corn bread, okra, cabbage, and drank plenty cold tea. Some sisters kept one eye slanted to make sure that their dish was being consumed. Ritually, they had prayed over their steaming pots, believing that if they didn't no one would eat from them. If vanishing food were any indication, all of them must have had a breakthrough. Some members made second and third trips to the serving table to pile on their favorites. They ate until they loosened suspenders, tugged at girdles, could hardly walk, or felt a nap coming on. Black people were famished for liberation, so they ate.

After the last of the desserts were gone, minds were set on the reason for the hour. At two o'clock the bell tolled and elders began the devotional prayer. Parishioners formed a line and filed into the church.

Agatta, Grace, Magdalena, and Zulime fell in at the end of the line. Each of them had courted the notion that the faithful knew they were *scarlet sisters,* but when members of the fold reached out to shake the hands of these well dressed women whom they presumed to be housewives (blessed housewives), the thoughts were banished.

The women of No. 51 went to a back pew. They stood in the tabernacle with its understated splendor. The ceilings were high with exposed wooden beams. A brass cross was emblazoned on the lectern. There were five chairs in the pulpit, the largest and central one belonging to the pastor; deacons occupied the others. There were two rows of pews that matched the dark cherry floors. The center isle was wide enough for fainting. Large arched windows adorned the stucco walls; today they were open to flood the sanctuary with an idyllic climate.

Agatta was surprised at how differently the church looked and felt from when she first visited. The people gave the edifice its sanctity. A sanctity that she wanted to share. She had reminded Sazar of

Luther's invitation; knowing that he had a curious streak, she hoped that it might get the best of him.

The energy inside was electrifying. Everyone was standing. Deacon Tyler's pure tenor voice sang, *"I love the Lord, he heard my cry!"* The congregation sang the refrain, *"Yes, oh yes."* People rocked with clenched fists lain across their chests. The deacon's range spilled into every crevice of the room. *"Long as I live, and trouble rise, I'll hasten to his throne!"* The congregation sang, *"Yes, oh yes!"* Those words were sung over and over, each time more passionately. A single verse summed every supplication that had ever passed their lips or rested on their hearts.

As the devotional song came to its close, the people moaned but they retained the same rhythm as when they sang lyrics.

Luther emerged from a door behind the pulpit. He wore a dark blue suit and a serene composure that must have staked him at dawn, for by now it was as much a part of him as his clean-shaven head. The absence of hair gave him distinction, made him royal. He approached the podium, placed his notes on the open Bible, and gazed out at his now silent flock. "Please be seated. I thank all of you for making this a fine Founders' Day. Ten years ago we started out with nineteen members, today our family is almost two hundred strong. Look how far the Lord done brought us."

All over the church people said, "Amen." Shouts were sparse and interjected by the coos of an infant.

Luther tugged at his bowtie as he cleared his throat. "So here we are in God's house, on his day, fulfilling his will. Ain't no place I'd rather be."

The congregation applauded. Deacons cautioned him, "Take your time." After turning through the Bible, he looked to his audience, and he found Agatta and her friends in back. He hoisted his shoulders and commenced to preach. "I want y'all to listen real close to this message, closer than you ever listened before. God deals in love. Since we claim to follow him, we too must deal in love. Sometimes we get so caught up in church house formalities," he placed his hand on the Bible, "til we forget that the Word of God is a guide for truth, knowledge, and most importantly—the Good Book teaches us how to live. The Lord wants us to live holy."

Clenching the podium, he thoughtfully examined the people; as far as he could tell he had their attention. "For a long time I held this message too dear to my heart to preach. I know that's selfish, but I'm human."

There was a soft chord of laughter from the pews.

"See this message comes from a passage that my mother used to read to me and my brothers and sisters. Turn to the Book of Romans. Read with me the thirteenth chapter, the eighth verse. 'Owe no man any thing but to love one another: for he that loveth another hath fulfilled the law'." Luther looked up from the Bible, drawn away by a ray of light in the middle of the church. An unexpected guest.

Sazar took a seat on one of the folding chairs near the door. He and Agatta usually spent Sundays together. He was somewhat perplexed that she chose to attend church (Luther's) first and see him later. Since he was seated behind her, he could keep an eye on her.

"Those words laid the foundation for my life," Luther's voice turned raspy. A deacon gave him water.

Someone shouted, "Take your time!"

Another encouraged him, "Speak! Speak!"

The women on the front pew fanned themselves restlessly.

"Each of us is a temple. A house if you will, for a mind, body, and soul. Without love and compassion your temple is on a shallow foundation. Without love in your heart, you are useless to God. But if you avail yourself to the Lord, he can fill you up with so much love til you can't keep it to yourself. Caring about people will come as naturally as breathing. Love alters circumstances. Love changes people. Without love your house is sinking in quicksand. Some of y'all houses made of stone; nothing can penetrate them. Some of you dwell in caves. Where there's no love, there's no light."

Luther threw his hands up, and stepped beside the podium. "The Master's love is pure and unmerited. To tell the truth, we could never be worthy of Christ's sacrifice. He loves without conditions. That's how we're supposed to love each other. It is by love alone that we can restore one another, heal one another, love builds the spirit up. Love is an unshakeable force. Anybody who's ever buried a loved one can attest that the love lives on long after the grass grows over the grave.

"I've known people who have never been loved; I mean really cared for. Their hearts fall into two lots: the hard heart or the broken heart. I've learned that you can't rush them to heal from either affliction. It may take years of just loving them just as they are—wounds, sins, and all. Eventually, love will soften the hard heart and piece the broken heart back together. We don't need spells or potions. That all consuming agape love of God's is all the magic we'll ever need. Ain't no hoodoo like God do."

He stepped out of the pulpit and strolled down the center isle. "Without love your soul ain't rested and you're cut off from God. Love is one thing that you have to give to get. A hard heart will cause you to miss out on some of life's greatest joys. A hard heart is a cold heart. If your heart is cold, you may have a pulse, but you're living dead."

Fans stirred like a swarm of butterflies in flight. People started to rest on their feet, shaking tambourines.

"Yes, a lot of y'all used to be coldhearted before you got saved. But look at some of us now, looking down on folks who remind us of yesterday. That same love that drew you in can draw somebody else in, if you dare to love. Love without judgment. Love without keeping score. I charge you to go out into the world and show love and compassion, no matter what the situation, no matter what the cost.

"Remember how Jesus met you right where you were. The crossroads, the low roads, the back roads, the ditches. The Lord was there to put his loving arms around you. That's his way of showing us that none of us is too far gone for him to reach. I pray that all of you go the way of holiness and reach out where you would have turned away."

Luther ventured to the back of the church. He ran a handkerchief over his drenched face. "Love . . . love . . . love. That hollow space inside that only God can fill. How does he love us? His love is sacrificial, supernatural. It's before this world and after this world. God's love is a deep, deep thing."

The pianist played softly. His fingertips crept along the keys, the ivory cried a dreadful plea: a song of slow rain falling to a doomed harvest. The freshman tones were unfamiliar to Agatta, but as the arrangement progressed, she recognized this music—it was Shorty's music. Now the tambourines rattled like incessantly falling coins. People tapped their feet and clapped.

Luther shouted, "Have mercy on love!" He danced. His movements started out jovial and carefree. Then he took a bow, waved his hands and shuffled his feet. Now he moved with precision. He stood up straight, elevated his shoulders, rocked from side to side and back and forth, looking ahead at something that only he could see. He stretched his hands out before him, sharing the dance but keeping the lead. The spectre whose waist he cradled could have been a woman. Yet Luther was not seducing this spirit, he was sacredly celebrating it. He danced as through he and God were alone together. Dance he did. He shut his eyes. For every one strut forward, he took two steps back. Tears streamed down his cheeks. He smiled a redemptive smile, his whole face was gleeful; at that instant, whatever he needed—he had. Then at full speed he ran the periphery of the tabernacle three times.

Shouts erupted all over the room. Praise manifested in diverse ways. Some people stood with hands lifted high, some wept aloud, some cried quietly, and some danced. There were those who sprung from the pews to shake violently, like an unshackled prisoner testing the mobility of newly emancipated limbs. Yet there were those whom the spirit led to be still and they were anchored in place.

At random Luther prayed and laid hands on people. Holy unrest went on for more than an hour. Then just as unpredictably as the spirit exploded into fruition, it came to its own mysterious repose. Freed of their omens, the scattered drifted back to their places. Except for the smallest of children who had slept through the visitation of the Holy Ghost, almost everyone was standing. Luther returned to the pulpit. "Those of you who are weary, troubled, vexed, in need of a blessing; come to the altar and give your burdens to Jesus."

Heeding the pastor's call, wayfarers progressed to the altar. So many came until the majority stood in the isles. "Everybody get on your knees wherever you are."

Agatta knelt down and rested her elbows on the pew, as did Magdalena. Grace and Zulime exchanged glances, unsure if they were willing to go as far. Then they noticed Agatta watching from the corner of her judging eye, so they complied.

Sazar stood up to leave, but not without a message to Agatta. She read his lips. He said see you later.

"Father, Father, Father. We come before the throne of grace, laying all our woes at your feet. Lord only you know all that we been through and all that lies ahead. We are babies in your loving arms. But Lord we are strangers in a strange land. It is you, only you that gives us strength to be conquerors. Surely we would perish if we look for help anywhere else. Help us to press our way. Help us to help ourselves. We are your people, and we will honor you from the rising of the sun to the going down of the same. Amen."

"Amen, amen, amen, . . . amen," they said, until the word thrived as an invocation in and of itself.

# 15

## Treasure

I *am* my beloved's, and his desire *is* toward me.
—Song of Solomon 7:10

Where did Sazar learn to love like this? Could this even be taught? These questions teased Agatta as she rested under the weight of her man. Warm and rapid, his breath sprayed her face. His kisses landed at random on her neck, chin, underarm, nipples. She could never predict where rapture might next transpire. He sent his tongue along her mouth, rousing the nerves in her lips to life. He tickled her navel then kissed her birthmark, coaxing a latent giggle from her. Romance was foolish. For whenever he showered affection on the mark, they both fancied that he could swallow her whole.

Wholly beside herself, she shouted, "*Whewwww!*" Her thighs shivered as his fingers perpetually explored them. She anchored her shoulders to the pillow, tossed her head wildly. Now her eyes were wide open, as were his. She drew him down, pressing his chest to hers. "Merci girl," he moaned. They rocked until ecstasy fled them.

Neither of them were afterglow sleepers. They were contemplators. He snuggled his face against her belly. "It's scares me that I never tire of you."

"Who needs a woman that he tires of?" She went to the washstand and splashed her face with cool water. Winking at him, she piled her hair atop her head in a bun. Her hands fell to the hollow of her hips. She gazed at the mirror and wondered how long she had left to look this good.

For seconds, Sazar closed his eyes before getting up to slide his pants on. When Agatta passed by, he stole a kiss from her shoulder and twirled her around before she fell back into bed. He glanced out the window before turning around as though he might approach the door; instead, he stood there stretching his arms. He looked at her again. She still exuded that girlish innocence and fragility that first captured him. No longer were those qualities necessary to keep him, yet the preservation of softness comforted him. Everything about her deserved to be loved, protected, and passed on.

He searched through a drawer, and retrieved a ring of keys. He unlocked the armoire to recover a strongbox. Along with the keys, he sat the box on her pillow. "Open up."

Neither eager nor indifferent, she followed his orders. Inside she found a red velvet pouch full of dollar coins and a roll of bills. She thumbed through the roll to find mostly 20s and 100s. "You buying more than new dresses."

"The passbook to your savings at Teutonia is there too. Two of those keys are to this house, your house. We'll change the deed Monday week."

"Well sir, I got my own cottage in Tremé. I reckon that makes me a bona fide queen of New Orleans."

"You're my queen. Don't ever bed down at Zulime's again."

"I haven't for some time. Seems I'm ill to any touch but yours."

"Good. We suffer from the same malady."

She turned over on her stomach, bent her knees, and swung her feet.

For the first time, he took a sobering look at the scar. True—it had drawn smaller than he had predicted. But it was still an unsettling relic left behind to caution him that his cherished one should be handled with care. "The ring is there too."

"Ring?"

"Mama's."

Quickly, she sat up, spilling coins onto the sheets and floor as she shook the pouch. Finally, the ring appeared. She slid the gold band on her finger; it fit as though it had been made for her. Agatta stretched her hand out before her then looked to Sazar.

He kissed her feet. "Whenever you're ready."

# 16

## Bravado Alley

He that hasteth to be rich *hath* an evil eye, and considereth not that poverty shall come upon him.
—Proverb 28:22

Women manipulate their bodies so many ways in pursuit of men's attention. At Dracon's they put on the best show in New Orleans. They raised skirts, lowered garters, and exposed nipples. The later the hour, the more brazen they became. They tickled men with feathered boas, and did perverted acrobatics on the bar. Women were desirable as long as men were in the mood for them. But if the fellas had gambling fever, feminine wiles could not compete with Bravado Alley.

The second story of Dracon's was reserved for those who liked to take chances. This story could also be entered from outside via a stairwell in back of the saloon. Dracon said he named the floor Bravado Alley because men liked challenging each other, they liked to win, and having something to lose made them feel important.

The rooms were relatively small. Each had three or four game tables and a manned liquor stand. The house supplied chips. Players were free to bring their own cards and dice. Every room had a single window, which usually stayed open to filter out the endless haze of cigar smoke and lessen the powers of body heat. Time and again, Dracon had threatened to blow the hand off of anyone who emptied spittoons from his windows. Yet occasionally when his back was turned, slime drenched unsuspecting alley travellers.

Though women weren't restricted by code, they seldom ventured to Bravado Alley. Indeed, with all the farting, cussing, and banging on tables, the environment wasn't particularly appealing to feminine company. So most women stayed downstairs unless they were cajoled to do otherwise.

Numa clutched Magdalena's hand, and whispered in her ear, "Baby, I need you." She pulled away. He circled her and captured her pouting face in his hands. "You my luck, girl."

"Really?" she giggled. "Then brother you need a brand new gris-gris."

"What's wrong with the one I got?"

"Numa, you're not lucky."

He pinched her chin. "I got the prettiest woman in the world by my side. My dear, I *am* lucky."

"You got the devil's silver tongue."

"And an angel to love."

She sighed with her hands on her hips. "You know I hate up there more than I hate gambling. Besides, I don't feel well."

"Come on now, be my luck."

"It stinks up there! Last time we left there, I scrubbed myself raw, and still stunk Bravado Alley."

"Tonight I won't be that long."

"You said that last time," she folded her arms, "and we stayed til morning. I like to fainted from that stench."

"Just a quick game. I promise. I don't play half as much as I used to."

"Why you keep company with such folks? I've seen all kinds, but none worse than what goes up these stairs."

"Mag."

"We better leave when I'm ready, else I'm going home by myself."

"Fair enough." Numa kissed her then rushed upstairs with her reluctantly trailing behind. "Hurry dolin'."

"Don't rush me. You got long enough to lose."

"Come on," he mumbled, locking arms with her as they went down the hall.

Though doors were closed, the escaping noise indicated players were in the heat of the game. The simultaneous shuffling of cards, dragging of chairs, and foot stomping accompanied a drone of voices. "Bartender" and "deal" were the only lucid communications.

"In here?" Numa led Magdalena inside the third room. "I promise, just one game."

She blinked repeatedly to relieve her pupils from the smoke that enveloped them. Fearing that her hair might harbor the musty smell, she caught it up in a bun. A stale taste crept inside her mouth as her stomach heaved. "Get me a drink." She looked around to discover that she was the only woman in the room.

Numa watched the color fleeing her cheeks. "You alright?"

"Yes," she answered, breathing rapidly. "Just get me a drink. We can't stay long."

"We won't." He scanned the room for a vacant table. There was one in the corner, just shy of the window; he guided Magdalena towards it, and flagged the bartender.

Dizzied, she followed, trying to avoid bumping into tables and making eye contact. Numa sat her down in the chair closet to the window. "Is that better?"

"Yeah," she answered with a lack of conviction that left him wondering if he would get to play.

The bartender approached them. "How you folks tonight?"

"Fine sir. Bring me a bottle of bourbon and a pitcher of water please."

Sitting sideways with her head pressed to the wall, Magdalena inhaled a stream of fresh air, and her stomach began to settle. She exhaled slowly and escorted her thoughts to the earlier part of the day; a day that she and Numa had spent together. They had taken the ferry to Algiers and picnicked with his Aunt Alice. She was spry, had a proclivity for gin, and confirmed Magdalena's suspicion that Numa had been a mischievous child. Alice treated her like family, and was quite impressed that her favorite nephew managed to snag a pretty schoolteacher.

Magdalena cherished days like today. Days when she and Numa held hands and talked. Days that made her feel loved, and chased away the feeling of being displaced. On such blissful occasions she saw the possibility of having a family, with babies and all. They had talked about that (Alice brought up the subject over lemon cake) on the way back to New Orleans, and she and Numa were of the same mind. Whenever that happened, his gambling became insignificant. So she sat at that table and dwelled on how good the afternoon had fared. The fact that she might have to subsidize him until his next hustle ceased to matter at the moment.

"Here love." He poured her a glass of water.

In one gulp, she consumed her drink. "More."

"Yes ma'am! But slow down. I can't have you in the privy when I need a stroke."

"I'll try."

"Hah! I feel good girl. I think lady luck got something for me tonight."

"I hope she gives it to you early."

"We can't rush her baby."

Magdalena sipped her water. She got comfortable in her chair again, and tried not to think about where she was; which was difficult enough to do, then there was an added distraction. Through half opened eyes, she saw a tattered black fabric hovering above rusted spurs. She elevated her gaze.

Dag neared their table. He tried to smile, but his efforts only exaggerated the crookedness of his face, and made Magdalena wince.

"You alright?" Numa asked, pulling a deck of cards from his vest pocket.

"I feel sick. Let's go."

"Just one game. Please baby."

She stood. "I'm leaving."

"No. Mag, honey it's too late for you to walk home by yourself. Bear with me baby, we'll leave together."

She flopped down in her seat.

Dag approached the table. Magdalena turned her face toward the window.

"Well, well. Numa, I thought we seen the last of you."

"No sir. I'm a betting man til I die."

"Do tell. I see you brought some fine luck. She got a name?"

Magdalena loathed Dag. The sound of his voice was coarse and dry. He spoke as though a fistful of rocks were lodged in his throat. Likewise, his voice mirrored his appearance; he was one of the ugliest men she had ever seen. Up close she could see the wild hairs sprouting from his nostrils, and the deep pits in his face. He was nightmarish, the sort she never wanted to see twice, or in the dark, or when no one else was around.

"Her name's Magdalena. Everybody calls her Mag for short. She don't say much, til she knows you better."

"Is that so?"

"What you say my man? We have a game?"

"If you up to it." Dag sat down across from Numa.

"Always."

"I'll make it easy for you," Dag said, waving across the room, "winner takes all—a two hundred dollar pot. One game. Every man throws fifty dollars in the pot. You pick the fourth man."

Cloud came over. "What you need?"

"Our old friend here up for a game. You in?"

"Sho'." Eagerly, Cloud took the seat to Dag's left.

"Jimmy!" Numa called out, snapping his fingers. "Over here, partner."

Jimmy Johnson was a short, heavy set, brown-skinned man. He had one of those faces; if Numa hadn't known him, he would have known someone who looked like him. But for most of Numa's life he had known him, because he had worked for Numa's father before starting his own carpentry business.

Jimmy swallowed the last drop from his bottle and rushed to the table. "What you got for me?"

"A quick game." Numa winked.

"What the stakes?"

"Every man sweetens the pot with fifty dollars. We play one game, winner takes all."

"I'm in." Jimmy took the chair to Numa's left.

Numa reached back and rubbed Magdalena's knee. "Angel on my shoulder."

Each man cast fifty dollars to the center of the table. Numa stacked the deck next to the cash. "Who'll deal?"

Each player drew a card. They drew four times until Numa turned over a jack and dealt the cards.

Magdalena grew drowsy as she watched the strategic movements of his hands flipping, folding, sliding. Precise maneuvers that supposedly insured fair play. Studying him reminded her of her clairvoyant grandmother, whom she called Nana, when she dealt the tarot. Both decks held the façade of good fortune or the omen of fortune less favored. The poker's ace or the tarot's tower, all cards were wild because they were left to that which could not be counted on—chance. Giving too much credence to cards of any sort usually led to doom. Grown people with their gambling and fortune-telling, same as children exhausting the fields for four-leaf clovers. She made up her mind to keep her eyes open as her man cut, shuffled, and lined the cards with expert precision.

Jimmy leaned back, casually puffing on a cigar, keeping one eye on the dealer. While Dag and Cloud conspicuously analyzed Numa's handling of the deck; neither of them touched their drinks. Cloud stared with his shoulders hunched and mouth gaped open. Dag planted his eyes on Numa's fingers and followed them wherever they went.

In clockwise rotation, Numa dealt five cards to every player. He stacked the rest of the deck beside the pot. "Your bet Jimmy."

"I bet three," Jimmy grunted, pushing three chips to the pot.

"Call three." Dag handed over his chips.

"Three," Cloud said.

Meeting Dag's gaze, Numa said, "Raise two," and contributed five chips.

"Call." Jimmy eased two chips to the pot.

Dag hesitated, squinting his bloodshot eyes. "Call." He slammed his hand on the table before clenching a pair of chips and tossing them in.

Cloud followed suit. "Call."

All bets were equal. Numa began the draw. "It's your ride Jimmy."

"Drop one."

Numa drew a card from the top of the deck and flung it to Jimmy.

"What you say Dag?"

Wiggling his tongue between the gaps in his front teeth, Dag smirked, knocked on the table, and shook his head. "No."

Cloud signaled that he was standing pat also.

"I'll stand with y'all," Numa said, casting the deck to temporary exile.

It was dark out, and the next day had begun. The crowds had thinned. Bartenders had to lead a few belligerent drunks out.

As for Bravado Alley, it was easy to tell the winners from the losers, especially the sore losers. A reaping hustler took his time exiting. He might even slide his chair back in place, or finish sipping his poison. Certainly he would button his coat, cock his hat, and set his sights on the next hustle. A loser groaned, backed away from the table in disbelief, put his hands on his knees, blew from his gut, looked the winner in the face long enough to be considered rude, then he finally paid up and left. A sore loser was a slave to his ego, and ego was highly unpredictable.

Magdalena pulled her watch chain and slid the timepiece out of her bodice; it was seventeen minutes past two. She refrained from coughing or sighing to get Numa's attention. Instead she reminded herself that if he won, she would not have to pay his rent for the next couple of months. Thus, she thought it best to let him concentrate. Restlessly, she shifted her weight to the other side of the chair.

The second betting round commenced. Jimmy fidgeted with his cuffs. Dag scowled. Cloud was drowsy and indifferent. Numa was zealous. "Y'all ready?"

"Wait a minute." Jimmy went to the bar and jovially skipped back to the table with a bottle. "How 'bout a drop?" He started filling glasses before anyone objected.

Numa rubbed his palms. "Your bet papa."

Between swigs, Jimmy said, "I bet seven."

Dag called, as did Cloud.

"Raise ten." Numa gave seventeen chips.

Jimmy turned his bottle up and beads of whiskey ran down the back of his hand. "Too rich for my blood."

"You mighty bold tonight." Dag made a fist under his chin.

"As a lion in his den." Numa responded.

"I'm dropping," Dag said.

"Cloud, what you gon' do?"

"Drop."

"Hah! Contender takes all." Numa showed his hand: 6-6-6-5-2.

"I'll be damned!" Dag pushed away from the table, stood, and leaned in Numa's face. "You bluffed!"

Jimmy intervened. "All's fair brother. That's the game."

Dag spread his cards, revealing a better hand: K-Q-J-9-8. "Let's go again."

"No. One game—winner takes all." Numa counted his winnings and tucked them inside his vest.

Grinding his teeth, Dag said, "Ain't nothing meant to be that easy."

"If you'd stayed in, you would've won."

"Umh, I should've known you was bettin' big and actin' cocky for something."

"To win."

"To bluff."

Stupefied, Cloud looked from Dag to Numa. He kept his cards facedown.

Jimmy put his hat on and shook Numa's hand. "Take care now. They'll be other games fellas."

"I ain't done with this one," Dag clenched his fists.

"I am. Goodnight all." Numa held his arm out for Magdalena, who was already standing. "Let's go dolin'." He nodded to Dag and Cloud. "Til next time."

The other game rooms were empty. Downstairs the chairs were on top of the tables. A few dreary-faced lushes remained at the bar. A barefoot maid went around turning out lamps.

Numa swung the door out and held it for Magdalena. Twirling the pink silk purse he had given her, she walked ahead of him. He presumed she was pouting. He laughed to himself. Fifteen hours in a necktie left him feeling confined, so he took it off and unfastened the top button of his shirt. "Hey! Wait for me," he called, hurrying to catch up to her.

"Why should I?"

"Cause girl, I'll take care of you."

Grinning in spite of herself, she waited for him. "I give you credit for one thing, you always know what to say."

He captured her under his arm; though reluctant, she fell into his embrace with little resistance. He counted the cost of forgiveness while she tallied the benefits of loving him. Their unspoken sums were alike: daybreak would find them in each other's arms.

# 17

## Secrets

Behold, I shew you a mystery; We shall not all sleep, but we shall all be changed.
—1 Corinthians 15:51

Zulime swelled with joy as her staff feasted at her table. She could not help herself; sharing breakfast with almost a dozen people made her reminisce about family gatherings back home in Baton Rouge.

The faces surrounding her made No. 51 home. Yet she could not help but wonder whose pillow absorbed tears that fell for these women? Whose hopes fell short because they were gone? Who prayed for God to watch over their daughter? their sister? their wife? their mother? Surely some families had no idea that their loved one had fallen into harlotry. Though it was true, Zulime could not imagine that some families didn't care what had happened to these women. The romantic in her always pictured happy endings for her girls; the realist in her stayed neutral.

She sliced into an omelette spilling over with plump sausage and ripe peppers, and took a bite. Sal outdone herself, she thought. No sooner than she lowered her fork, the cook approached the table with a coffeepot in hand. "Anybody want more?"

Though Grace had scarcely eaten at all, she held her cup up for more chickory.

"Grace, I reckon you watching you're figure," Zulime teased.

"The longer I stay fine, the better. Besides, I'm not hungry."

"Can I finish that for you?" Magdalena asked.

"Help yourself."

"Good girl. Waste not, want not." Zulime pushed her plate aside. "I'm sure all of you found a surprise under your door this morning. Ladies, spring is almost over, and we had a good season. You earned your bonuses."

They raised their cups in salute to Zulime then lined up to thank her.

"You must be one of the sweetest women in the world." Grace kissed Zulime's hand.

"If I'm one of the best you come across, that's fine by me."

"You are."

"I'm one of the luckiest for sure."

"Yeah, she sweet alright." Magdalena hugged Zulime. "Thanks Mam."

"Don't spend it all in one place."

"No one place is that good."

"What about that place called Numa?"

"Sweet as can be, but the devil got her tongue. I'll see y'all after while." Magdalena left with the others.

"You seen Agatta?" Zulime asked.

"Yeah, earlier," Grace answered. "On her way to the room. Want me to go get her?"

"No. I'll go."

Agatta pinched a burning candlewick, parching her fingertips. She stood in the center of the attic, reassessing its order, and channeling her own. Satisfied that her spirit had received the sustenance of solitude, she decided to leave. She closed the door behind her and paused before descending the stairs. At the end of the corridor a sunbathed window seat invited her to rest.

There were enough people out and about to make the quarter look busy. Saturday morning was a time to tie up loose ends left over from the week. She, however, found herself grateful for having fewer loose ends to tie. The windowpane warmed her shoulder, and the street doings below gradually ceased to hold her captive.

"What's on your mind?"

Agatta turned to see Zulime, whom she had not heard come up the stairs. "I'm pleased to report—absolutely nothing."

"You get your gift?"

"Yes, but I don't know why you gave it to me."

"You still pay me."

"So, you know."

"You disappear when you're regulars call."

"You don't stop me."

"They still find pleasure under this roof. I respect Sazar's feelings and yours too. I know it takes time to let go and move on."

"You don't miss nothing."

"Only what passes me in sleep."

"You don't sleep much."

"I knew this day was coming, and I'm happy for you."

"That's strange. I didn't see this day coming. When I came to this house, I never thought about leaving."

"You were a child. You didn't know you'd wind up here. But surely you didn't see yourself growing old here."

"I don't know Mam. I suppose pondering the future ain't my thing."

"Well, you have a man who loves you to share the future with."

"That, I do. Sometimes I think I'm gon' lose my mind loving him so much, but I don't care. I didn't know I could feel this way."

"A woman learns all kinds of things about herself, just when she thinks there's nothing left to discover."

They went down the hall, where the door to Magdalena's crib was open. She stood before the mirror, gathering her dress in a wad, which she held at her lower back. She turned repeatedly as though playing a game of *look and see,* but her concentration was of the serious kind. She fussed some more before smoothing out her dress, completely unaware that she had briefly been under surveillance.

"Wonder what Mag studying herself for so?" Agatta asked.

"It's been almost two months since she hung out rags," Zulime softly replied.

*18*

# Evil

Because of the voice of the enemy, because of the oppression of the wicked: for they cast iniquity upon me, and in wrath they hate me.

—Psalm 55:3

Sazar gave the paperboy a dime, and went to the back of the grocery store to the cafeteria window. He ordered two stuffed fish lunches then went out to the courtyard. Water spouted from the mouth of a life-sized cherub. Plump goldfish swam amongst water lilies, free from danger since their spectator had outgrown knee pants. For there was a time when he would have reached in, captured a shimmering inhabitant, and gazed upon it as it slithered briefly in his grasp before returning it to the water. Today he settled for a seat on the bricks.

He rearranged the *Daily Picayune,* moving the sections that interested him to the front. He was engrossed in the follies at City Hall when a double shadow cast itself on the page.

"Afternoon, Mr. Jorda. Suppose it don't hurt to find you, if I'm looking for Numa." Dag sucked his teeth.

"Why are you looking for him?" Sazar folded the newspaper. "As I recall, all of his debts to you are paid. Lest my memory fails me, I paid them."

"Your memory's fine, but your friend racked up some fresh debts. Now they overdue."

"Are these honest, betting, lost the game debts? Or, we're broke, so let's go shake down Numa Sabatier debts?"

Dag looked at the ground, then with one eye on Sazar, he answered, "Honest debts."

"You're lying. Numa told me that he beat you a few weeks ago at Dracon's."

"That wasn't our last game."

"Last I heard of." With his gaze on Numa's adversaries, Sazar eased the paper under his arm and stood. "If you can't get clean clothes and a bath out of your hustle, you need to try a sunup to sundown."

"That's easy for you to say. Your reapings come sweet and easy, cause you look like the law."

"I reap cause I'm not a damn fool." Sazar went to the counter, collected his order, and strolled out to the street.

The afternoon air was welcoming. The day was warm, but a cool breeze floated off the Mississippi. He walked the tree-lined streets of the Tremé. The palms he found intriguing; the Chinese fans, windmills, and especially the banana palms with their delectable green convex fruit. The magnolias, however, captured his sentiments, for they were a safe harbor from the treacherous sun. As a boy, no matter how hard he played, afterwards he could rest on an aged trunk to sip a soda, and catch his second wind.

Block after block, a distinct garden adorned every house. A pageant of flowers, each genus uniquely perfuming the air, and painting the landscape with an incomparable tint. Stems flourished from common soil in close proximity, yet without infringement. Not one blossom waned due to another's splendor. No rose lost its rouge because a lily decided to bloom. Vines grew wild and strong along the iron lace, expanding naturally, never stymieing one another. Growth and glory operated seamlessly as natural phases in the life cycle, unless the subjects were human.

Sazar found himself at a crossroads: St. Bernard and St. Claude. He was equal distance from his home and Numa's. The food will get cold . . . Agatta's waiting . . . I can check on Sabatier later, he thought.

Tossing the dice on the porch, Numa derived as much pleasure as he did shooting marbles when he was a youngster. He stretched his legs and hoisted his behind up to see if he had sat on any mulberries; the fruit tree was one of three mature trees that nestled the bungalow.

He tapped his feet on the steps, and rested on his elbows while he tried to make up his mind whether to go inside for another cup of coffee or to take a siesta in the shade. He rolled the dice and swooped them up as he started inside. Then, though several blocks away, he thought he saw Dag and Cloud. Squinting, Numa ducked until he was certain that his nemeses were headed his way.

Dropping the cubes, bruising his foot, and leaving the door unlatched—he fled. He ran behind his house, and through a neighbor's garden. With his undershirt soaked, he slowed down to catch his breath once he was well out of harm's way.

Magdalena gradually awakened from a sound sleep. She lay on her stomach with her face resting on a numb arm. She resolved to stretch, search for Numa, and find out the time of day. The curtains were drawn; since time failed to influence Numa's sleeping pattern, there was no clock in the bedroom. If the neighbor's rooster had crowed, she had slept through its summons. The house was still, leaving her to assume that Numa was on the porch. She called, "Numa! How come you didn't wake me? I bet the whole day gone cher!"

She kicked the covers away and sat up expecting him to come through the door with prizes: a dashing grin, playful affection, and promises. She sighed at the exhaustive amount of energy required to lure him from what he called "feeling out his luck."

"Numa!" She fell back on the bed, and daydreamed a spell. Then she sat up again to hold her face in her hands; when she removed them, she saw a stretch of sunlight in the hall, and a male silhouette fell onto the glow. Oddly, he was slow-footed. "Ah, 'bout time." She fluffed a pillow and eased it behind her shoulders. "I been calling you for the longest. You carrying on something terrible this morning. I hope you keep it up," she giggled.

"I reckon I will."

A knot formed in Magdalena's gut. She prayed that she was having a nightmare. She wanted to pinch herself but fear kept her still. She dared not even look near the doorway; instead she stared at the foot of the bed and told herself that the intruders would get scared and flee. Also she tried to convince herself that Numa would arrive in the nick of time. Shortly thereafter, the facts confronted her: she was wide-awake, the intruders had nothing to fear, Numa was gone, and she was alone with dangerous men.

Dag entered the room. He touched her leg from her ankle to her thigh, where he squeezed until the flesh turned pink. She tried to cross her legs; yet that amused him. "Sugar, this ain't no way to welcome me." Abruptly, she drew her legs in and sat up. He sat down in front of her. She moved away from him until her back was against the headboard, but his cape still touched her toes. "How come he leave you all by yourself?"

"He's here."

"No he ain't. Nobody here but me, ol' Cloud there, and you."

Cloud stood off to the side of the doorway with his back to them, nervously stirring his hands in his pockets.

"Numa might've ran up the way, but he'll be right back. Y'all better go." The desperation in Magdalena's voice betrayed her. She turned away from Dag. When he tried to goad her into looking at him, she resisted.

She weighed the possibilities of escaping. If she sprung from the bed, maybe she could get away.

Her gown, however, was long and loose, so she might trip and fall. The greater obstacle was Cloud standing guard. She could scream, she *could* scream. Would her cries be heard? Would screaming worsen her plight?

She invested substantial energy in trying to envision herself exiting the house and breaking into the streets; but such a vision evaded her. Then an opportunity presented itself. Cloud had slipped out of sight. Bent on a miracle, she tested her luck at hastily fleeing the bed; only for Dag to pull her by the hair before her feet touched the floor.

He slapped her hard enough to leave a stinging imprint on her cheek. Now he pulled her close to him as she trembled, and licked her ear. "You biggity heifer."

Despite an immeasurable desire to stave off tears, Magdalena began to cry. Though too afraid to wipe her eyes, she clenched the sheet to divert attention from her aching cheek. But there was more torture in store; his rank tongue craved her neck and face. She feared fainting from Dag's odor, he smelled like rotten meat.

Next, his hands—they went haywire under her gown while he attempted to kiss her. In protest she stiffened, and the more he tried, the more resolute she became. Then he gripped her neck with both hands. She struggled to break free, and kept her lips turned in. Unexpectedly, he loosened his hold and snickered as she backed away from him. He tugged at her toes, and rubbed her feet all over. Her feet were soft but cold; he tickled her soles while searching her face as though he anticipated some trace of arousal or amusement. “We gon’ have a good time,” he said.

She stretched out the foot that Dag seemed to favor, and allowed him to get comfortable. He took his hat off, rested on his side, and resumed the foot rubbing. Seeing that his guard was as far down as it was likely to get, she took a chance and kicked him in the face. With him disarmed, she cleared the bedroom and aimed for the front door, and had almost made it when he yelled, “Get her!”

Cloud caught her from behind and dragged her back to the bedroom. “Let me go!” she wept. “Please let me go!” She fell to her knees.

Dag knelt down behind her, and felt under her gown some more.

She sobbed as he combed her spine, and derived pleasure from her turmoil. He tousled her hair to the side and kissed the back of her neck. He rocked slowly, releasing a series of prolonged groans. There they were; one in Elysium, the other in Gehenna.

Magdalena lamented the tears falling to her lap, expanding a damp circle of sorrow. She looked up, and there stood a voyeuristic Cloud, a dumb servant awaiting instruction from his master, a master who was oblivious to his charge.

Holding her hips, Dag pressed her to his hardened crouch and ravenously licked her bare shoulders. Lukewarm and foul, his saliva trickled down her arm. A button snapped, and his stench waxed even stronger. He pulled her gown up and had his way.

I wish I was dead, she thought. To assuage the pain, she wrung her hair and bit the inside of her lip until her tongue tasted salt.

Dag thrust. “I hope you bleed, if you can.”

Blood, blood she had. Magdalena turned and spat on him.

His eyes flew open as the sanguine spittle settled on his nose and cheeks.

She pulled her gown down past her knees and edged her way near the door. Coughing frantically, she desired more than anything to get on her feet. Beyond the door she saw only the seam of Cloud’s britches. Her cough subsided. She was afraid to look behind and see Dag’s position; though she desperately wanted to know his proximity to her. She asked herself, How many times have I come and gone through this door? She tried again to picture herself escaping, but still could not. The harder she tried, the bleaker the outlook. So bleak, that instead of wailing from the kick of Dag’s boot, she rolled over and absorbed the blow assailed at her back.

He straddled her while she scratched and slapped at his face; her hands were no more vicious than those of a hysterical child. At first he smirked at her feeble defense then his impatience erupted. “Here,” he said, throwing his cape to Cloud, “tie ‘em up.”

Magdalena twitched and bucked as Cloud harnessed her hands above her head. She squeezed her eyes shut and prayed for darkness to triumph. All the while, she wondered where Numa was?

She wanted to wipe herself clean of Dag, who finally slumped away from her. "Whew!" he said, pulling his britches up. "No wonder that ol' gal Clovis so rich!"

Though her thighs, hips, and the space between ached, she resigned her body to numbness. A body that she inhabited, yet presently did not own. In fact, the only part of her that thrived was her convulsing belly; she would have given much for her belly to be still. Instead, she held her breath to keep form vomiting. She lay there as her inner warrior slowly retreated, knowing that the battle had a ways to go.

Staring lecherously below Magdalena's navel, Cloud asked, "How 'bout me?"

Dag wiped his sweaty face with his shirttail. "How 'bout you?" he said, and traded places with Cloud.

Involuntarily, Magdalena looked at the cloud, and her memory ricocheted to Nana's theory of signs and wonders: Cloud comprised half of the storm.

He dropped his trousers and bent over, giving no attention to whether or not he was within range, nor to the possibility of loosing his footing due to his cuffs being under his heels. Wholly transfixed by the pearly skin, loose turban of shiny hair, and eyes the color of the sea; he could not believe that she was real, let alone captive. He leapt on top of her. With all her might she tried to feign an out of body experience, a device that had operated as second nature at work, but now failed under duress. Finally, she liberated the terrible croak that she had held in thus far. “Ahhhhh . . . no, no, please.”

“Shut up! You want me to string you?” Dag snapped.

Having resolved that clamor was her only viable weapon, she screamed again. “Help! Help! Help!”

Dag untied her hands and bound the cape around her neck. He tightened the noose, leaving her to gasp for air as Cloud continued his bestial dance.

Her moans were reduced to whimpers. She twitched uncontrollably and made futile motions to free her throat.

Cloud’s dance approached its finale when a snickering Dag drew back his reach and mercilessly strained the noose in concert with Cloud’s last severe thrust.

Magdalena’s eyes bulged while her fingers, though weakening, still pried at her neck, and her grunts soon wasted to faint susurration to nothing at all.

Alienation now loomed as eminent as the torture had. For the last time, the cruel question vexed her, Where is Numa? I’ve always been there for him, she lamented. Then time hung in the balance; though not without design, much like the way it operates when a falling leaf circuits a tree before descending to the ground. The physical agony subsided. In fact, a merciful cocoon spun itself about her. Someone else was there, someone who comforted her. A beckoning entity, whom she could sense but not yet see. Magdalena was uncertain about accepting the invitation until the spirit of the innocent wandered off to greet the host; even then her decision was not resolved. She levitated above the slain woman as the wicked withdrew from her. They marveled at how pale the slain woman's face had become. Next, they broke lamps, pillaged through dressers and under the mattress, which they tossed on the floor.

The innocent returned, rested at Magdalena's breast, and cooed lovingly before turning east, where the host stood. Magdalena bid the slain woman good-bye. She cuddled the innocent and they went with the host.

It was sundown when Sazar and Agatta approached Numa's house. The front door was wide open. With trepidation in his voice, he said, "Stay here." She paced the porch and held her breath as he twice called, "Numa!" When he cried out again to no avail, she went inside.

The house was thick with spirits: rueful, sadistic, pure, holy, and redeemed.

She found Sazar in the guestroom, and walked ahead of him to Numa's room. She dropped her purse and fell to her knees near Magdalena. "Numa!" Sazar called again; this time the sound was harrowing.

He came to Numa's room, but stopped short of the door. He could not enter because there was no place for him in that space—that sacred space. He had permission to witness the rites and await clearance until after the invisible wall of fire had burned itself out.

Agatta wanted to touch her friend and fix her to where she wouldn't look so bad. Yet the heaviness in her heart had transferred to her hands, rendering them immobile. So she beheld her ruined sister until the shock settled.

Magdalena was soiled. Black, purple, and blue shades of torture laced her neck. Her open mouth was full of filth. Hair covered half of her face, partially masking her expression. Agatta believed that the face of the dead might disclose truths that were otherwise incommunicable. Moreover, she needed to see the face for the sake of seeing.

Life crept into her fingers and they ventured to work on Magdalena. She stroked back the hair, revealing a sad, frightened, open-eyed face. She peered intently into the once bright blue eyes that now appeared more indigo than she would ever care to recall; although she knew good and well that she would never forget. After all, the power of evil hinged on the potency of its imprint. Agatta eased the lids over the pitch blue wells. She touched the cruel colors on the neck, forever staining her fingers. She then gently pulled Magdalena's gown down to her ankles; she never did like to show too much. Now the situation gained a semblance of normality; though that wasn't what she sought. She endeavored to give her friend some measure of dignity. Lastly, she took her handkerchief out and cleaned Magdalena's mouth.

Now Agatta was free to address Sazar. "Fix the mattress."

"What?"

"So you can put her on the bed."

"Dolin', we have to go to the police."

"Fix the mattress. Put her on the bed." She crawled aside, clearing the way for him.

He returned the mattress to the bed. To nail his grief down, he breathed long and hard before gathering Magdalena in his arms and laying her down and folding her hands across her chest. He took a step back. Somehow distance made it easier for him to view her. To himself he resolved, no more. "Let's go."

"I'll stay with her."

"No. You won't"

"Why not?"

"They might come back. Besides, we have to give account to the law and tell the others."

"Lock the door."

"I will." Sazar went to the back porch and retrieved a key from a can hidden underneath the house.

Still, Agatta stood watch over Magdalena. Seeing that she would not leave without solicitation, he took her by the hand. "Let's go."

# *19*

## Confession

I said in my haste, All men *are* liars.
—Psalm 116:11

News of Magdalena's death and the details thereof traveled fast. In whispers and drunken babble alike, it was reported that her lover's foolishness had led to her demise. Murdered tramps were not rare. Dead whores surfacing in alleys were commonplace, sometimes the river coughed them up, or their mutilated corpses were found in steamer trunks. For prostitutes murder was an occupational hazard; incidentally, their unidentified remains made interesting cadavers for students of medicine.

The irony in Magdalena's death made it sensational. She had worked in a sweet house for a madam who had never lost a girl to violence; moreover, she was not slain at work. Talk of a bounty kindled even more interest.

Eager outlaws waited for Zulime to put a price on the perpetrators' heads. In dance halls, saloons, cigar shops, jails, and assignation houses, the conversations about blood money were serious and inquisitive. Gunmen, seasoned and green alike, had their ears wide open.

Bordellos profited from the scandal. Hustlers tipped graciously with one parting request, "Sugar, if you hear anything 'bout the price for them fellas that kill Zulime's gal, you come straight to me with the news." The less ambitious relied on the pillow talk of easy washerwomen and barmaids.

Some speculated that Zulime had already hired a gun, and that most likely he was someone that she knew well.

While tongues wagged, Zulime kept her plans private. Though she accepted Sazar's account of the events that led to Magdalena's death, she still wanted a remorseful confession from Numa.

Zulime and Sazar barged in on Numa to find him shirtless and asleep at the kitchen table. "Numa." Sazar tapped him on the shoulder.

"Huh?" he responded without raising his head. "Who here?"

"Come on man, it's me Sazar and Mam Zulime. Look here."

"Y'all go on," he said groggily. "I'm still sleep."

Zulime stepped forward, bent over, and spoke into Numa's ear. "We ain't going nowhere til we get some answers from you."

"Answers. What sort of answers?"

"You know damn well what sort of answers," she said.

"Where were you?" Sazar inquired. "Did you see anything? Hear anything?"

"Naw."

"So Mag was by herself?"

"Where were you?" Zulime asked.

"I must've stepped out for a minute."

She pinched Numa's forearm. "Look at me."

"Woman, cant' you see I'm tired?"

"All I see is a pitiful man sleeping off a drunk."

Sazar sat down across from Numa. "I ran into Dag and Cloud that day, and they were looking for you."

"That day? What day you talking about?"

"Tuesday."

"Tuesday?"

"July 19, the day Mag died."

"Oh."

"They must've come here, and found her—alone."

Numa lifted his head slightly. His vision was blurred, so the only thing that stood out was the glare from Sazar's belt buckle. "You got it all figured out." He rubbed his eyes. "What you want from me?"

Zulime spoke before Sazar could. "The truth."

Sazar rapped on the table. "Look at me, if you can. We've known each other all our lives. Man, we were boys together. Please, be straight with us. Now it was before noon when I saw Dag and Cloud; if they headed here directly, you were home."

"You don't know where I was."

"You never leave the house before three; except on Fridays when you step out early to go to the barber."

"You timing me now? Need I remind you that you're not my father?"

"Need I remind you that I couldn't handle the shame?"

Zulime scoffed. "I must have been stalk raving mad to think that talking to you would tell me any more than I already know." She stooped down and spoke into Numa's face but he refused to lock eyes with her. The venom of her words, however, he could not avoid. "You don't even care enough about Mag to tell the truth. You don't even care enough to be angry. I've come across some sure enough scoundrels in my time, but brother you bear the palm."

Numa stood and turned his back to his interrogators. He wanted to run, yet he could think of no place to go, so he put his face to the wall and sobbed.

"Well, there you have it—a deceitful bastard will weep every time." She started out of the kitchen. "Let's go."

Trembling, Numa dropped to the floor. "No matter what y'all think, I couldn't help what happened. Mag was right, I'm not lucky." He rolled around erratically then finally came to rest on his back. "I'm sorry . . . I'm so sorry Mag . . . it should've been me . . . please forgive me."

Zulime scrutinized him; though he was half naked, she failed to see what it was about him that Magdalena couldn't live without. "*Sorry* won't do her a bit of good."

"Well, it's all I got!"

"You sang that song so long til you honestly believe it."

"It's the truth!"

"No, the truth is you a lousy hustler, who loves to sleep late, live easy, and keep his hands soft."

"You don't know! You don't know me old woman!" Numa cried out, and then he faced Zulime. "I saw them coming this way, so I ran!"

"Who *did you* see?"

"I was gon' come back."

"Tell me who."

"It don't matter."

"Oh, it matters much."

"You can't change nothing."

She pounded on the table as her voice enveloped the house. "Tell me now!"

Wringing his hair as his chest heaved, Numa confessed. "Dag and Cloud. I didn't know they would kill Mag . . . that never crossed my mind."

"How could it, when you only think of yourself?"

"Nobody loved her like I did."

Shaking her head in disgust, Zulime folded her purse and tucked it under her arm. "I knew you for a loser, and figured you for a fool. I should've known you'd be a coward cause you love chance so much. You too scared to stand on a sure thing; too yellow to stand your ground with the devil. Umh, I've known all kinds of women to love just about anything called *man,* but I never knew a woman to love like Magdalena Marie loved you. Money! Hah! Freehearted as she was, she would have paid your debts. But you, let her die for them." Numa pained Zulime's heart so much that she found herself unable to look upon him any longer. As for words, he had none to satisfy her; he could offer no explanation that might aid her in making sense of her friend's death. She looked about the house where Magdalena had taken her last breath, and found evidence of her life draped over the small kitchen window. The ivory curtains were made of lace that Magdalena had purchased on one of their Canal Street excursions. The intricate pattern of long winding vines and flower buds outlined with tiny pearls that the vendeuse had referred to as "vines and roses." The material could have easily been a fashionable veil or lovely christening gown. Few accoutrements equaled the ethereal beauty of lace, but one tear and the entire article would be ruined. Loveliness and fragility frequently went hand in hand. Zulime suppressed the urge to holler; instead, she said to Sazar, "I'll be outside."

Jittering, Numa hid his face between his knees. His callers had come much too early. They had taken him by surprise before he had time to slip on the suit of charm. The had come before he could sustain his train of thought. They had come before he had a chance to take a swig of confidence from his flask. That he couldn't make them see that he was the one without luck and love tormented him. They had arrived early enough to capture him in his purest form—the troubled man.

He lacked the fortitude to address Sazar, who had said little during this encounter. Whereas he was relieved for not having to endure double jeopardy, he was perplexed because Sazar's silence left his motives obscured.

Finally, he asked, "What are you going to do?"

"I can't do nothing. I got nothing."

"When you had everything, you didn't know it."

Numa waited until he heard the door close, and then he wept himself to sleep.

# 20

## Mourning and Rituals

Also *when* they shall be afraid of *that which is* high, and fears *shall be* in the way, and the almond tree shall flourish, and the grasshopper shall be a burden, and desire shall fail: because man goeth to his long home, and the mourners go about the streets.

—Ecclesiastes 12:5

Sir Coudriet sat tall driving the State Coach through the quarter. Zulime rode silently, secretly wanting to detour. Having never made funeral arrangements, she didn't know what to expect, and feared that she could not handle viewing the deceased. The last time that death had visited her it had transpired via her womb, and Zulime's mother had cleansed and dressed the stillborn, Eliza, so that when Zulime held her, she looked like an angel asleep. After she had cuddled her long enough, Zulime's father placed the infant in a small wooden box and buried her to the east of his house; in the same spot where his grieving daughter had courted her beaus and played patty-cake with her sister.

In a glimpse she acknowledged that Coudriet had indeed aged some in the nearly two decades that he had worked for her. He was tall, dark, and still lean. Instead of etching creases in his face, age had favored him with refinement and an air of wisdom; his deeply set eyes now set even deeper. She was glad that he had stayed around for so long, and she almost started to ponder all the people that had come and gone through her life, but she stopped short of allowing the myriad of faces to take shape since she could at present mourn but one.

Agatta kept her head down. Her face was bloated and her eyes were red. For the last several days her hair stayed in a braid. Today she wore a plain white calico dress with a round neckline. She looked like a schoolgirl. Zulime glanced at Grace, who upon hearing of Magdalena's demise, retreated to her room and spoke only when absolutely necessary.

Wanting to break the curse of silence, but uncertain of the appropriate discourse, Zulime chanced a question, "You took them a gown?"

"Yes," Agatta mumbled.

"A new one?"

"Yes."

"Good."

"We took everything she needed," Grace added.

Agatta reached over and patted Zulime's knee. "She'll be put away real fine."

Grace sighed and folded her arms. "I hope they have her looking like herself."

"I'm sure they will," Agatta said.

"You wired her people?" Zulime asked Grace.

"Yeah, I sent word but I don't expect they'll come or respond. Mag sent money home every month with a letter. The money never came back; neither did thanks."

"Sometimes blood harder on you than anybody else." Zulime looked ahead, not to anywhere in particular, but simply because she was unwilling to confront Grace's distress. "We here for her—that's enough."

"It might as well be."

Coudriet slowed the coach and drove up the carriageway to a white neoclassical structure. He hitched the horses to posts then helped the women out of the vehicle.

They were greeted by Xavier St. Ours, a third generation colored undertaker, at St. Ours Mortuary. His ruddy complexion, grey eyes, and red hair gave him presence; however, earnestly caring for the dead had left him devoid of warmth. Sustaining the legacies of his grandfather and father had banished all remnants of his own individuality. In a stylish black suit, he was a somber and dignified figure that women imagined presiding over their coffins as opposed to their beds. "Afternoon, ladies," he said, "come right this way." He led them to the sitting room. "Would you all care for tea?"

"No, thank you." Zulime replied for the three of them.

"Very well then. Please make yourselves comfortable. My father will be out shortly."

While they waited, a wall covered with funereal photographs kept them occupied. The coffins were stunning; from the tiny, white, flower laden eternal cradles to the regal black, chrome studded caskets of colored aristocrats. There were a few images of simple pine box coffins. Large portraits captured memorial services that looked more like parades than home going ceremonies.

The gallery immortalized grief in all its complexities. There were photographs of little children saying good-bye to their parents. Widows made intriguing subjects. Young lovelorn widows wondered how, when, and where romance and commitment might visit them again. Aged widows appeared either bereft or relieved; regardless of how they felt, they kept a handkerchief close by. There were also pictures of widowers. A young widower usually held an infant who had cost him his wife and hollered for her milk. Old widowers stared into open graves and caught tears in their hats.

The elder, Narcisse St. Ours, approached them. Though he bore a strong resemblance to his son, he was better looking and his disposition, though reserved, was not stifled. "Hello ladies."

"Hello, Mr. St. Ours." Zulime rose.

"I'm deeply sorry for your loss. Please, come right this way." He guided them down a brief corridor, past several rooms. He opened the double doors to a small chapel. Velvet indigo paper covered the walls. The pale blue marble floors gave the impression of stepping onto a pool. A soft glow illuminated from flambeau-style wall sconces, and candles flickered from the silver torchères that flanked the pearl grey coffin. Arrangements of chrysanthemums and white roses surrounded the departed.

Zulime walked alongside Narcisse, unaware that Grace and Agatta had halted at the vestibule. When she approached the altar, she realized that they had stayed behind.

Haunted by the memory of a brutalized Magdalena, gradually Agatta went forward. A starkly different recollection accompanied Grace's reluctance: one of her and Magdalena laughing and splitting an orange. Midway to the altar, Agatta stopped to await Grace, who inevitably joined her. They locked hands just as Zulime turned to them.

They moved gracefully as though partaking in an innate dance to some clandestine drumbeat. Her mind's eye played a dastardly hoax on her by placing Magdalena in their midst. The three of them had always struck Zulime as sisters by bond. Had they not found each other, their journeys would have suffered tremendous voids. She thought it utterly implausible to behold the surviving two without seeing all three.

Finally, side by side, Agatta and Grace viewed the deceased.

The gown's high collar hid the strangulation marks. Agatta folded over a few rows of lace to see if she could detect any bruises; they were not easily discernable because the morticians had performed a stellar job cosmeticizing. She smoothed out the collar and focused on Magdalena's face, where she was confronted by the brutal truth: the dead didn't appear to be sleeping or at peace—they just looked dead. Her hair was right; parted down the middle and unbound to rest on the pillow. Her hands were folded across her chest, and they symbolized life for Agatta; for they had stretched out and led her from the alley; they had tended her on sickbed; they had beautified her crown and glory. Magdalena's hands had nurtured Agatta; thus, they had a life all their own, so she mourned them separately.

Grace and Zulime viewed the casket lengthwise from a comfortable distance, and neither scrutinized its contents. Nevertheless, Agatta examined the dead closely.

Narcisse stood with a hand behind his back and the other extended toward the coffin. "Madam Clovis, is everything to your satisfaction?"

"Yes, indeed. You did a fine job. She looks . . . like herself." Zulime nodded. "Don't you think so, Agatta?"

"She looks fine," Agatta answered, still fixed on Magdalena. "Her hair is pretty; she would like it."

"It would be hard to make Mag look like anything less than an angel," Grace added.

"She was a prize." Now Zulime looked at Magdalena's face. Under the weight of grief, her chest caved in and her shoulders sank. The tears that she had held for days now surrendered to the gravity of sorrow, and she could not recover her handkerchief soon enough. She patted her eyes and cleared her throat. "Life don't spare many of those." She folded her arms and withdrew to mourn privately. "You did well, Mr. St. Ours, as I expected."

The undertaker followed her outside the chapel, leaving Grace on a pew and Agatta at the altar. "How did you and Mag meet?"

"Not long after Leo died, one afternoon, I was sorting through fabric at a shop on Canal, she came up and we started talking. It was a love affair at first sight. I felt like I had known her forever. We got on like sisters. Just being around her made my way sweeter. We worked out of different holes at the time, then after being friends for about two years, we started working for Mam."

"Umh, when I met y'all, I knew whatever y'all had—I wanted."

"Is that so?"

"Yeah."

"I reckon you got it. I suppose this life looks real fine early on, then you find out that it comes with things."

Agatta sat down next to Grace. "Everything comes with something."

# 21

## Rest

But go thou thy way till the end *be:* for thou shalt rest, and stand in thy lot at the end of the days.
—Daniel 12:13

Black crepe hung on the front door of No. 51. Inside the mirrors were covered. There were no lighthearted conversations or music and the house was virtually empty.

For reasons that Zulime could not decipher, she went to Magdalena's crib and stood before a closed door. A door that had so often been open. Open so that Magdalena could greet everybody; open for girls to come and borrow things; open for visits. Now, all that remained were things left behind by a kind soul.

Zulime had ordered the door closed; now she lacked the fortitude to enter. There was something on the other side of that threshold that unnerved her. Fear seldom surfaced in her; when it did, it came with every regret, sorrow, and slight in its tide. This time was no different.

Madam Gorée had been Zulime's friend and mentor. Her heyday began to flounder as Zulime's started to flourish. The old woman grew envious, as is usually the case when the protégé outshines the master. Their final visit had been a strained one. Madam Gorée's tongue had spewed acid; she told Zulime that if she ever buried one girl, she would bury plenty. At the time, Zulime dismissed (or so she thought) the comments as the ramblings of a jealous hag whose vision was fleeting and whose judgment was skewed by narcotics, booze, and rendezvous with opportunistic fellows. Her once gilded bordello descended into an opium den.

Up until now, she hadn't realized why she clung to the ideal of never losing a girl. She had tucked Gorée's words away in her heart, and there they colonized to govern her every move; which is exactly what the shrew desired. Never mind the fact that her girls were grown women with independent lives and free wills; nevertheless, that's how fear operated—illogically.

With that revelation, she saw no reason to explore inside Magdalena's room. So she went downstairs, cursing herself for lacking the energy to move swiftly. With curtains drawn she sat alone in the parlor. She hoped sleep would befall her, but her frenzied thoughts vacillated between her dear friend and the mother she missed. She thought of retrieving the keepsake from her beloved mother, but her will was too weak to go combing through a chest, so recollection alone would have to suffice.

The day that Zulime had left home, her mother wept profusely. After she dried her eyes, she placed a saturated handkerchief in her daughter's hand. Zulime kept the memento neatly folded in a trinket box and stored away in a cedar chest. Sometimes when the longing for her mama was maddening, she pinned the tearstained cloth to her breast or laid it upon her pillow so that she could inhale its scent as she awaited sleep. To this day, on Christmas and Mardi Gras, she bestowed white handkerchiefs on her customers and colleagues. She figured everybody at some time or another shed tears.

A key turned in the front door. She sat up and fluffed her hair out.

Agatta propped a black parasol against the wall. "Mam, you been in here all morning?"

"No, just a little while."

Glancing around the dark room, Agatta eased her weight onto the arm of a sofa. "I never knew this house to be so still."

"Death slows things."

"Not without love."

"Love, a blessing and a burden."

"Yet some of us choose to do so."

"That's one of the few choices we get."

Light footfalls came from the hall as Grace's voice echoed through the house. "Coudriet coming around; the hearse already out front." She peeked inside the parlor as she pulled a veil over her face.

"Is everything like I ordered?" Zulime asked.

"It most certainly is."

Zulime looked around trying to recall where she had placed her hat.

On the mantle Agatta found a trailing veil, hat, and purse. "Here you go."

Improvisation proved challenging for Zulime as she tried to tuck stray hairs under the hat without the aid of a mirror.

"Here," Grace said, taking a couple of pins out of her own hair. She pinned Zulime's wayward curls down, stylishly propped the hat, and then draped the veil. "Now that's better. You look right fine, Mam."

"Hats never was much my thing; they for tall women like y'all. But I have to look dignified to bury the dead."

"Well lady, that one suits you," Agatta said.

Grace added, "Mag would be mighty proud."

Zulime smoothed out her dress and took her purse. "I reckon that's what counts."

They left the parlor and stepped out into the midday heat to behold an open show of compassion that ran for blocks. From balconies, porches, and curbside, the people of Dauphine Street saluted them with white handkerchiefs. The women of No. 51 were awestruck and humbled by the hundreds who honored them and the departed; they stood spellbound vowing always to remember this pageantry of goodwill and solidarity.

Under the glow of daylight, a coffin draped with flowers shone like sterling as sympathizers steadily added to the bouquet. Wearing a top hat, the hearse driver sat square-shouldered. In his charge were jet horses whose heads were dressed with elaborate grey plumes and grey fringed fabric clothed their backs.

Once the women boarded the coach, Coudriet took the driver's seat, and signaled for the hearse driver to proceed. They rode past throngs of people fanning white handkerchiefs on Dauphine en route to St. Louis Cemetery No. 1.

The drive was a short one. Brevity was a favor since they were really ready to lay Magdalena to rest. They arrived at their destination before they had settled into their seats good.

Zulime, Agatta, and Grace went to stand among the others from No. 51. While Sazar, Numa, Coudriet and Shorty along with Albert Sigur, a former suitor of Magdalena's, and his twin, Emmett, carried the coffin.

Luther cleared his throat and spoke softly. "Blessed are they that mourn: for they shall be comforted. Beloved, we are gathered here to mourn the passing of Miss Magdalena Marie. Now, I had the privilege of knowing her for only a short while. Let me tell you, I learned right early that she was a bold as she was beautiful. She had a kind heart; there was nothing that she wouldn't do for a friend. She was a blessing, one that we will cherish forever. It is well that she has returned to our father, for her work here is finished. Though we will continue to love and miss her, we can rest assured that the Lord comes for what belongs to him. We have but a short while to live among one another. When that time is spent with love, we gain in depth what we sacrifice in length. Love is the equalizer. Our sister, Magdalena, knew how to love."

Luther held his hands high. “Father, give us strength in the hour of weakness. Make us whole where we were once broken. Amen.”

Everyone turned their attention to the grave as the pallbearers lowered the casket into the earth. As did the others; Numa shoveled assiduously, remaining silent and keeping his gaze down.

Zulime had purchased the plot for coping over a decade ago. She gazed at the mound of dirt certain that she would rest there also, along with any other soul from No. 51 in need of a resting place. Her charges regarded the grave as another facet of her benevolence, transcending from temporal to eternal. The coffin began to disappear under the soil. Zulime moved in closer for a last look. Her girls followed. Shoulder to shoulder they stood.

# 22

## The Substance of Dreams

Now a thing was secretly brought to me, and mine ear received a little thereof. In thoughts from the visions of the night, when deep sleep falleth on men.

—Job 4:12-13

Agatta stood at the bottom of the stairwell and watched Zulime in her study flipping through papers, making notes here and there. She decided not to interrupt, but instead to go upstairs as another girl entered the study. She listened to their conversation and visualized Zulime's gestures according to the inflections of her voice.

Slowly, Agatta ascended the stairs hoping for Shorty to play the music that belonged to him; music that she had sanctioned as her own. She wanted that old organ to open up and address the fury inside her that words failed to explore, let alone explain. That music helped her to live; now she needed it to help her work.

She had cleared out her own crib. Presently she faced the task of packing Magdalena's belongings; a chore set aside for her and Grace, though they had yet to appoint a time. She hadn't seen Grace at all that evening so Agatta figured she would start sorting Magdalena's things on her own. She could stay the night since Sazar was away visiting his mother.

She went to Magdalena's room and placed her hand upon the door as though feeling for proof of life. She went inside where toiletries sat on the dresser just as Magdalena had left them and the mirror remained tilted to same degree. She struck a match on the wall and lit the lamp. Light wavered about the room until the flame found its balance.

A photograph of the four of them sat on the dresser in an oval frame. She held the picture for a moment and then carefully sat it back in place. The image had been snapped on a mild spring day when they had ridden the ferry to Algiers and back. As they were leaving the dock, a dwarf with a candescent smile approached them and insisted that he photograph them. He said they were the most bewitching ladies he had ever seen and swore that he would follow them home unless they honored him with a pose. Whereas none of them were given to flattery and Grace and Agatta were bent to keep on walking, something of his charm persuaded Magdalena and Zulime. Tobias Sparrow was his name. He took off his coat, set up his lens and captured them for all time. Afterwards he handed each of them a business card and guaranteed they would be pleased. It was Magdalena who had eagerly gone to his studio to purchase the photograph.

Agatta continued to eye the picture as she undressed. Then she pulled out several drawers until she found a stack of neatly folded lingerie. As she sorted through the articles, she came upon a small pink gift box. Inside she discovered a tiny gold cross on a short delicate chain. With tears filling her eyes, she sat on the floor clinging to the necklace. After she wept for its intended, she returned it to the hiding place.

She reclined on the floor and stared at the ceiling with its chameleon shades and shadows cast by the flickering light. She began to calm. Somewhat easier, she breathed and felt better for having cried. She lay there as the dancing flame illuminated the headboard, where a bed gown hung on a post. She went over and spread the garment out. With its hue of champagne, balloon sleeves, low neckline, Empire waist and silk, she recalled it well. The gown was one of Grace's creations. Vividly, Agatta remembered Magdalena's fitting. They fussed like children that day. Magdalena wanted a close-fitting gown; Grace, on the other hand, insisted that the garment move about her form, not "wrestle with it." Somehow they found a compromise.

Agatta buried her face in the gown, wallowing in its softness and whiffs of honeysuckle. She went and stood before the mirror and held the gown to her body; she felt compelled to slip it on. As the hem billowed down to her ankles, she let out a sigh of liberation. The puffed sleeves gathered at her wrists like soft blown bangles. With an image of Magdalena in her mind's eye, she viewed herself. Her body was taut; Magdalena had been voluptuous. The contrast left her feeling like a girl playing dress up in her mama's raiment. Nevertheless, she claimed the item as a keepsake.

Before turning out the lamp, she opened the window then knelt bedside to talk to God. With head bowed and eyes closed, she wondered what to say. The Lord's Prayer came to mind, but not to mouth. Though aware *that* prayer would cover all things, she wanted to speak from her soul so the words had to be mined from there. Often when she yearned to make explicit supplications, they battered her spirit so until they almost became too harrowing to voice. But she managed to face her demons for the beasts of burdens they were, and talked to God as best she could. "Lord, I do not know what my tomorrows may bring. I only pray they're better than my yesterdays."

She eased into bed, covered herself with a sheet and curled up in a fetal position. She hoped to doze off quickly, but she was restless. It was a warm night and she had only covered herself for security's sake; though the sheet was no rival for her beau's arms. After some tossing and turning, she cast the covering off and rested her face on the edge of the pillow.

Out of boredom she listened to Shorty's music. He wasn't playing the torrid notes that she longed for. Instead he played gay melodies. Eventually her eyelids grew heavy and her limbs relaxed. She slept lightly at first. Slowly, she fell into a deep sleep. For the longest time it was vacant slumber until an image evolved.

Darkness was the backdrop. Then something of contrast floated onto the pitch-black canvas. A feather? A leaf of paper? Whatever it was, it moved whimsically. A tenuous article that caused her concern. Subconsciously she feared that the very air through which the object moved might blow it to shreds. Momentarily, the item disappeared, only to resurface shortly thereafter. Now its maneuvers acquired deliberateness. Its matter gradually came into focus as it flitted about a few times more. It was a veil now accompanied by a voice, a melodious voice. *I wear the crown . . . I live forever . . . forever . . . forever . . .* A silhouette manifested. *I live forever,* the voice said again and again. Every time the concluding word of the declaration was uttered, the outline procured substance. Waving hands appeared first, and next the hair. Agatta recognized the kindred spirit before the entire body formed and the veil lifted. Unmarred. Glorious. It was Magdalena.

Agatta wanted to call out to her, but every time she braced herself to make a sound, her words were bound by the deafening silence of sleep and the abyss between perception and reality. Her heart beat ahead of its normal timing as she jerked restlessly while struggling to speak her piece to eternity. To no avail, for her psyche was a ring of fire from which her affirmations could not escape. The verses spun and spun, burning that they might rise. *Stay . . . I'm so sorry . . . I miss you . . . thank you . . . I love you . . . always . . .* Lacking a medium of escape, the words erupted to break her sleep.

She awoke dizzied and troubled to the redolence of unfamiliar flowers. Questioning her vision, she placed her hands atop her head and grimaced. Solely to feel the fluttering of her eyelids she blinked then hastily sat up. For at the foot of the bed was an apparition of Magdalena. When the door opened, she vanished.

"Did you see her?" Agatta asked.

"No, but I feel her." Grace paused and glanced about the room before consoling Agatta, whose face she wiped with the garment she held. "Remember this?" She spread a dress the color of pewter between them.

"Where in the world did you find this?"

"In the armoire. I came in here the day after just to feel close to her. When I ran across this, I couldn't leave it behind. I wanted something of hers that was *ours* too."

"She wore this the day y'all found me."

Grace sat where Magdalena had. "Yes, she did. Umh, that girl was mercy come to life. She fed every hungry soul that came her way. Folks never had to ask her for nothing. If Mag saw a need, she met it."

"Both of you met mine for sure."

"I suppose we tried. We hoped you had somebody to go to. We could tell that you had been loved. But even after you started talking, you never mentioned a place or your people. We never meant for you to become one of us."

"There are worse things to be than a trull."

"Like what?"

"Cruel, unloved, lost forever."

"There's nothing worse than sacrificing my body. I learned to live with it, but I never made peace with it."

"After seeing my folks killed, I began to question the value of a body since it was so easy to rob of life."

"Why didn't you let us take you to the orphanage?"

"I didn't want to meet any more strangers. At my age, I wouldn't have been there long. Besides, I figured if this work didn't kill y'all, I could try it."

"You were pure. You bled."

"I had never known a man, but I saw the devil so I wasn't pure."

"Still, this life has a way of catching up with you."

Agatta turned backwards to lie in Grace's lap and cover herself with the dress. "We've been caught. Now we have to look further up the road."

Grace tickled Agatta's scalp. "Sister Rochelle used to say that life is a series of peculiar movements."

"Amen."

"Did Mag say anything?"

"Yeah, in my dream she kept saying 'I live forever.' "

"She came to let us know she's alright."

"I want to live forever."

"Me too, but not like this." Grace moved from under Agatta and stretched out. Before long they fell asleep with Magdalena's dress crumpled between them.

# 23

# Discord

A brother offended *is harder to be won* than a strong city: and *their* contentions *are* like the bars of a castle.

—Proverb 18:19

Enthusiastically, Numa strutted up Villere on his way to visit Sazar. The sun burned the back of his neck left sensitive by the barber's primer and razor. He had sucked all the cinnamon out of the toothpick between his lips, but it still felt comfortable in his mouth. He ran his hands down in a pocket fattened from a recent card game. Prosperity was in the air and blowing his way. He was one of Magdalena's life insurance beneficiaries; the other was her grandmother.

It felt strange leaving Holiday's on a Friday without Sazar, who now got his hair cut on a different day. The barbers never let his new appointment slip, and Numa dared not ask.

Without a friend, or the open ear and soft voice of a woman who loved him, he was lonely. Today he simply hoped that he had given Sazar enough time. He tossed the toothpick and stepped up to the porch. With some reserve, he raised the knocker and rapped lightly on the door.

Sazar answered.

Posturing confidence, Numa leaned back on his heels. His palms were sweating, so he was glad that Sazar didn't reach for his hand. "What you say, partner?"

"I'm doing fine, and you?" Sazar came outside and sat on the swing.

"Looking for my next stroke."

"Stroke?"

"Yeah, you know me. I'm always on the lookout for luck."

"Some things never change."

"No sir, and they don't need to. Especially when my game's rolling. Lately, all I see is lady luck."

"That's one way to stay blind to your faults."

"Faults?" Numa hung his head down for a moment. "Last time I checked, you had some too." He propped his foot on the swing. "Oh sure! You read, use big words, but you're still a pimp—albeit a polished one."

"True. But a dreamer and a coward, those I'm not."

"Come on, I'm as much man as you or any other fella."

"When? On some private holiday from being yellow?"

"How in the hell can you call me on the carpet? You built a fortune off women's backs."

"I don't breed whores, I groom them. I love and rescued two."

"Look, you got your hustle, I got mine." Numa held some cash out. "I come by to make good on some debts."

"You stopped by here to check the weather. You best hold on to that blood money cause it might be some time before you find another woman to love you as much as Mag did."

"So it comes down to this. For over twenty-three years, we been close as brothers. Now all of a sudden you blaming me for all my troubles, and looking down on me as you go." Numa folded his arms and stepped off the porch. "I'm not like you. Always knowing way, having my way."

"Making my way. Troubles, well I've seen my share. Some of them I created, some I didn't. But only a glutton for punishment keeps fashioning the same vexations."

Numa turned his back to Sazar and looked to a trail of shade winding through a tree grove west of the house. A frog sprinted up the path followed by a pair of excited small boys.

"You plan on settling the score?"

"I'm no soldier. I figure it's best to leave well enough alone."

"You figure it's easier."

Numa reached up, picked a cherry and tossed it in his mouth. "Pity me for thinking I could make amends. I'll see you around."

"So long." Sazar watched Numa make his way up the walk until he faded off into the distance. Feeling a greater sense of relief than regret, he eased back in the swing, and rocked slowly.

# 24

## Farewell

For the Lamb which is in the midst of the throne shall feed them, and shall lead them unto living fountains of waters: and God shall wipe away all tears from their eyes.

—Revelation 7:17

The women of No. 51 congregated for a morning feast. They were all present. In remembrance of the dead there was a place set. With heads bowed, they joined hands and awaited Zulime's blessing. Despite the present silence, for the first time in a long time, an irrepressible spirit of optimism dwelled among them. "Father, we thank you for this meal and pray that someday soon we will break bread with Grace again. We wish her well, and ask that you guide her safely on her journey. Amen."

Tightly, they clenched hands before saying, "Amen."

As the food went around the table, inquiries as to how well Grace liked her parting gifts were made. They had showered her with gloves, hats, stockings, and cash. A dozen bolsters of fabric were ready to be shipped as soon as she secured a space for her boutique.

Grace looked wistfully at every face present. "Thank you all so much, for everything." She sighed. "The best part is anytime you come to Galveston, you have a place to stay. I'll have plenty of room and good food." She reached under the table and squeezed Agatta's hand. "Girl, I'm gon' miss you, but you come whenever you want. Don't bother sending word. Just come."

"Alright," Agatta said, solemnly.

"Don't be sad. I love you, whether near or far."

Zulime added a drop of cognac to her coffee before standing. "Grace Lorin, I hope and pray whatever you lay your hands on prospers. Of all the bridges you may cross and forget, don't be afraid to come this way again."

Grace rose placing her hand on Agatta's shoulder. "Lady, no matter where I go, I'll never forget this place. You, all of you, have been my family. I been missing y'all ever since I made up my mind to move on."

"Take good care of yourself."

"I will. And I'll send sketches of my best styles. So from now on, Galveston is the best place to buy a fine New Orleans dress."

Zulime raised her cup as the others joined her. "Farewell."

Coudriet had loaded Grace's baggage at first light. Unencumbered, she eagerly hopped into the carriage unassisted while he helped Zulime and Agatta aboard.

The morning fog was still thick as the streets began to people. As they rode, Grace attempted to recall if she had packed all of her belongings. She soon decided that if she had forgotten anything, it wasn't that important. What mattered more was for her to etch as much of New Orleans as she could into her memory. So now she acknowledged the details of landmarks and monuments that she had once taken for granted.

Coudriet pulled into the train station. The women walked Grace to the railcar that would take her to Texas while Coudriet collected the bags and followed.

Grace glanced at her ticket. "I'm gon' make a good life for myself."

Zulime embraced her. "Til we meet again."

"Thanks for everything, Mam."

"You're welcome. Send word as soon as you get settled."

"I will."

Agatta came forward. "I—" she started. "You—"

"Speak your heart," Grace urged.

"You already know."

"Tell me anyway. Hurry, fore this train take off without me."

"As much as I'll miss you, I'm glad to see you go in peace."

"Oh, Agatta. The world can't take that from us."

"I love you, Grace Lorin." They held each other, and then slowly withdrew.

Over the sounds of horns and whistles, the conductor called for all passengers to board.

"Good-bye, girl." Graced stepped on board and took her seat by the window. Jubilantly, she waved to her friends. The brakes released, screeching loudly as the locomotive moved down the tracks. When her exuberant smile journeyed off into the distance of destiny, Agatta and Zulime waved no more.

They walked up the platform. The fog had all but vanished, and a lovely day emerged. They told Coudriet to go on, for they preferred to walk.

# 25

## Born Again

Bring my soul out of prison, that I may praise thy name: the righteous shall compass me about; for thou shalt deal bountifully with me.

—Psalm 142:7

Outside a bountiful fig tree bore purplish-brown fruit as plump as dumplings. Sweeping against the shutters, the lush green leaves and thick branches coaxed Agatta awake. Reassured by the light of day, she lay nestled in Sazar's arms. She moved in closer to feel his breath on her neck, his knees pressed to the back of hers, and his heart beating into her backbone.

She observed the bouncing figs and decided to pick some and take them to Zulime. She wiggled a bit and her movements roused Sazar out of sleep. He yawned and extended his limbs. "You're awake early. Troubled mind can't rest."

"Neither can a thinking one."

He touched her birthmark, awaiting a smile; when she didn't, he pinched her nose. "Are you well?"

"As well as I can expect to be."

"I promise when you least expect to be, you'll be very very well." He got out of bed and slid his pants on.

"Draw my bath while I take a lil' nap."

"Why so early?"

"Church."

"Luther's?"

"Yes."

Agatta stood in the tub while Sazar opened a bottle of soap that smelled of roses and poured a few drops into the lukewarm water. When she eased down into the bath, he drizzled soap onto her hair. Dexterously, he massaged her scalp and lathered her tresses. In his hands she was as pliable as a lump of clay. She closed her eyes as tension fled her muscles, and sighed blissfully.

"You falling asleep on me?"

"No, just dreaming."

"Dream on." Carefully, he poured water over her head and watched the suds drip down her body. He untangled her curls with his fingers first and then combed her hair until it fell slick and radiant.

"You must want me to stay?"

"I want what you want."

She sat up straight while he bathed her all over lovingly and patiently the way her mama used to. Though the water cooled, her pleasure was unbroken. He went to the cistern and filled the pitcher again. Measuredly, he poured water down her torso. This time with each splash something inside of her was irrevocably changed. Long embedded strongholds of rage, grief, and hatred diminished. Initially nothing occupied their vacancies until peace took up residence where the bitter exiles once dwelled. Then an astonishing serenity overwhelmed her, causing her to shiver at first and numb her moments later.

Afraid of alarming Sazar, she kept her eyes shut to suppress the tears of unspeakable joy. But like opened floodgates, they would not be contained, so she splashed water on her face and wept undetected. With every teardrop she felt more alive. When she cried no more, she was new.

Sazar took Agatta's hand and helped her to rise before wrapping a towel around her. She went alone into the bedroom, where he had lain out her attire. She took a seat at the vanity and was stunned by the difference she saw in herself.

He came in and stood behind her. "You best hurry if you don't want to be late."

"I have time. You be here when I get back?"

"I might step out for a paper. After that, I'm home."

"Go now, so you can see me off."

Sazar walked along Villere and crossed at St. Louis. The Tremé was alive with fellowship and play. People gathered on front lawns and porches to socialize and catch up on the happenings of the past week. For some a drink of strong coffee or a quick chew of tobacco provided the boost of energy needed to trim hedges or shine their Sunday shoes. Little girls sang nursery rhymes and boys played hide-and-seek.

Although Sazar owned properties in Algiers and bayou country, Tremé was home. For him the neighborhood captured the very essence of New Orleans; specifically, black New Orleans. Given to occasional wanderlust, he had visited monumental cities and islands in Spain, France, Brazil and the Caribbean. All were spectacular in their own rights. Yet New Orleans was still his grande dame. A distinct vitality pervaded the Crescent City with its manifold vestiges of West Africa. The city was a testament to colored people's resilience and genius. While the contributions of transplanted Africans existed elsewhere, here they were everywhere. Black gifts had indelibly touched the architecture, food, music, and people of New Orleans.

Some called the place the city that care forgot. If this were so, surely grace and grandeur remembered. Having witnessed the exploited lives and stifled identities of colored people in other parts of the world, New Orleans was a place apart. For even during slavery, there were free black property owners, scholars, physicians, artisans, and entrepreneurs. He was not blindly romantic regarding his birthplace, he was well aware of its racial tribulations, yet he treasured its various reflections of Africanness. I'm proud of my people and this place, he thought.

Cavinee's Grocery had its usual crowd of patrons gathered out front drinking coffee and enjoying jovial conversations. Sazar grabbed all of the loose change from his pockets, gave it to the paperboy, and took a copy of *The Weekly Pelican.*

The cover story was the debutante ball, featuring a cadre of young colored women curtsying in lavish white gowns. A stark contrast, the lower left caption read: Notorious Hoodlums Found Slain Near Swamp.

That, however, was not news; save for the fact how soon they washed ashore. Surely that wagon wheel was heavy enough to weight them down; something must have disturbed it, Sazar concluded. It perplexed him how a man could be both stupid and evil. Cloud had drifted into the bushes seeking Dag; for fear that he was pissing too long. He was shocked to find his leader stretched out with his throat slit open. Hence, Cloud did not detect vengeance lurking in the moonlight. When he felt the strong arm across his chest and the blade at his ear, well, it was his turn.

Sazar folded the paper, glanced both ways, and dashed across the street. He walked a block or so before he sensed someone giving him intense consideration. He hesitated to seek the source of the attention, and walked another block before curiosity claimed the better of him. Ultimately, he found himself gazing in the direction from whence came the energy to discover Viv. She and Abby were across the street going the opposite direction. They carried traveling bags. Though Abby seemed not to notice him, without words, he and Viv communicated intensely. She disclosed the whole of what he knew in part.

She forgave and was grateful to be forgiven. After a season of tumultuous relations, they would move on and know nothing of each other's futures.

Their only solace would be memories, and the likelihood of crossing one another's minds during capricious afterthoughts or bouts of senility. Viv looked away as Sazar watched her and Abby fold into the crowds.

He returned to find Agatta waiting in the parlor. She looked lovely and refined in a pale blue dress. "Was I gone too long?"

"At all is too long." She winked. "You made good time."

"I could walk you."

"No, thank you." She picked up her purse and Bible. "I'll be fine."

"Alright, lady." He kissed her on the cheek. "I'll wait for you." He watched her from the vestibule. After she passed the hedges, he went upstairs to oversee her from the balcony. Whereas he could not systematically categorize his feelings regarding her spiritual endeavors, he understood the necessity of sovereign security. He was all that she needed of a worldly lover; though it was the eternal lover that allowed him to be so. In the end, it mattered less how God drew her or which messenger he sent.

Perched high as a falcon, he rested his elbows on the rail while she made her way up the street. While not physically alongside of her, spiritually he was right there with her—pressing her on. After all, she was his portion, his rib, and someone he could cover.

The syncopated cadence of fervent tambourine shaking spilled into the street. Not every lyric of the devotional song was perceptible over the moaning and shouting. Agatta, however, discerned the content about tribulations. The words triggered a cluster of memories without respect to chronology. Every recollection waxed poignantly as she began to hear a chorus that belonged to her alone. *You don't have to carry your burdens forever. There's grace enough to cover you. Another day or a hundred years from now, I want to spend it with you. I live forever. I love you whether near or far. You're enough like the sun, moon, and crops.*

The affirmations were a symphony held ransom, orchestrated for release when she had grown sufficient to hear. After emboldening her, the voices scattered that she might heed her own.

*My hands are by my sides. But I got a drum beating down in me. My God is Good.*

# About the Author

Cathy Clay was born in Houston, Texas. She graduated from the University of Houston with a bachelor's degree in Creative Writing and earned a master's degree in English from Texas Southern University. Her critical literary reviews have appeared in scholarly publications. Currently, she is writing her second novel and a collection of short fiction.